A TABLESPOON OF TEMPTATION

a Recipe for Love novel

KELLY COLLINS

BOOK NOOK PRESS

Chapter 1

DANIELLE

Danielle Morgan needed more than one breath of courage to exit her SUV. Today she needed two. There was no telling what waited beyond Trish's door. Last weekend it was Gene Horowitz; Danielle's surprise blind date. A date she was not prepared for.

Two weeks ago, she walked in on kitchen sexy time between Trish and her husband Rob testing out the strength of their new granite island. Right then, she vowed to never eat at Trish's unless it was takeout that went straight from the delivery person's hands to the coffee table.

Before Danielle could knock, her best friend opened the door and greeted her with a big smile. It was her I've-got-something-up-my-sleeve look.

"You better not have another one of Rob's cousins waiting for me." She turned, thinking she still had time to get away, but Trish took her elbow and pulled her inside.

"No one's here but Rob."

"Is he decent?" Danielle cleared her throat. "Meaning, is he dressed?"

Trish laughed. "Decent ... no. Fully clothed ... you bet."

Thank the heavens because there wasn't enough bleach to get that kitchen scene washed from her memory.

"You ready to go?" Trish picked up her purse from the hall table and looked over her shoulder. "Honey, I'm leaving."

Rob rushed around the corner and kissed her long and hard.

"It's not like she'll disappear forever. We're only hanging out for a few hours." Since her bestie had found love, their girl time shrunk from several nights a week dining out and watching movies to a few hours on the weekend. She didn't begrudge Trish's happiness. It was simply that Danielle was lonely. She wanted love. Instead, she got visiting rights to Trish.

She spun around and left the lovebirds on the doorstep to say their goodbyes.

Back behind the steering wheel, she waited and waited and waited.

Five minutes later, Trish skipped down the walkway like a teen after a tryst at Lookout Point. Her lips were red and bee-stung while her cheeks heated with a rosy blush.

"Sorry about that. It's a special day—our three-month anniversary."

Danielle rolled her eyes. "Tell me it's special when you hit your three-year anniversary. I hope his kisses still make you weak in the knees."

Trish dismissed her with a wave of her hand. "You're so jaded."

"I'm allowed to be." She squeezed the steering wheel harder and watched the blood drain from her fingers. "Don't forget that on my three-month anniversary, my husband wasn't running to give me a kiss. He was in room 301 banging Ms. Bancroft."

"Not all men are like Chris."

Danielle looked at her blissfully happy friend. "You're right. I can't punish every man for his infidelity, or his stupidity, or his complete disregard for anyone but himself. I should blame myself for being so impulsive. Who marries a guy after a month of dating?"

"We do. And sometimes it works out." She cocked her head to the side. "Look at Cinderella. She got the prince after one dance, and one day you'll hear the name Chris and say, 'Who'?"

"Let's hope." Seeing Trish happily married made Danielle happy, but it also made her miss the times when there was a man to warm her heart and her bed. "What are we doing today?" She pressed the ignition button, and her car purred to life.

"It's Swap Meet Saturday in Cedar Bluff." Trish bounced in her seat like a kid with front row seats to her favorite band.

"Thank God, I feared you'd set up another intervention."

Trish twisted to look at her. "Gene wasn't an intervention. He was a—"

"A disaster. The man wouldn't even look me in the eye, and you know how I feel about that. It's a sign of disrespect or dishonesty. Besides, he had bigger breasts than me."

"I can't speak to the man boobs, but Gene is shy, not dishonest."

"They say the eyes are the windows to the soul, and since I never saw his, I'm certain he's soulless." She drove out of Trish's neighborhood and turned onto the highway to Cedar Bluff.

"He's got a soul. He also has an astigmatism and that makes him self-conscious."

"Too bad he didn't have another *ism* like magnetism. The man was as exciting as a wet sponge. If this is what my dating life will be like, I'll pass. How could you think I'd be interested in him?"

Trish let out an exasperated breath. "You're going to give me an aneurysm with your criticism. Cut me some slack. I'd never met him, but Rob said he was nice and decent looking."

"If you like trolls."

"Okay, I promise no more blind dates."

They pulled into the parking lot of Cedar Bluff High School and exited the car. "You need to promise to stop meddling in my life," Danielle said.

"You don't have one unless you call working around the clock a life. You never take time for fun. You know what they say ... all work and no play—"

"Keeps me out of bankruptcy. I'm saddled with debt, and fun doesn't pay the bills."

"Fine. What's happening with the big takeover?"

"Argh, they're starting with the sweeping changes already—instead of The Pines, it's called Luxe Resorts."

"Ooh, sounds posh."

They entered the flea market and walked down the first aisle.

"Sounds scary to me. First, the name goes and next, the staff."

"You're good at your job. I don't imagine you'll have much to worry about."

Trish would never understand financial fear. She came from money.

Something caught Trish's eye, and she took off like a dog after a bone.

Danielle chased her, grateful she dressed in sneakers and jeans. "What are you looking for?"

"Inspiration." She held up a lamp with a shade faded by age and bartered with the owner until she got him to take five dollars. After the deal wrapped up, she asked him to hold it until she finished her rounds.

At the next vendor, Danielle picked up a heart-shaped box and opened it to find nothing but lint and dust. Would her hollowed-out heart look the same inside?

Trish snatched the box from her and set it down, leading her to the next seller who had cross stitch and paint by number kits by the hundreds.

"You're thirty-five, not dead. Look at me." She stomped her foot to get Danielle's attention. "I found love in my thirties."

"I found it too, and all it got me was an empty bank account and heartache."

Trish lifted a cross-stitch of a lady surrounded by cats. "If you're not careful, you'll be her."

Danielle plucked the kit from her friend's hand and set it down. "Never. I'm allergic to cats. I'm good with my life the way it is."

"You work and sleep." Trish shook her head and moved them along.

"And take field trips with you, which is all the fun I can handle."

"Your life should be more. Maybe a hobby would be good." Trish turned around and headed back to the craft table. "Cross-stitch could be fun."

Had her life turned into TV dinners, cross-stitch, and *Murder She Wrote*? She'd only started watching that show to see if she could figure out a way to murder Chris and get away with it. But she realized the killer always got caught.

"If I agree to try a new hobby, will you stop setting me up with trolls?"

Smiling, Trish said, "Yes."

Danielle searched the nearby vendors for anything to get Trish off her back. Spotting a box of cookbooks with a five-dollar tag, she hurried over. Trish knew Danielle couldn't boil an egg, so it was a believable attempt at a hobby.

"I'm getting this." Feeling victorious, she paid for the books and smirked.

Trish picked up the top one. "*The Beginners Guide to Baking*." She let out a laugh that shook her entire body. "I can't wait. The last time you "baked" a cake it cost you fifty dollars from Connie's confections."

"There was no way I was showing up empty-handed, and no one needed to know I bought that cake."

"My mom still thinks you're the most skilled cake baker in Pitkin County."

Danielle lifted her chin. "What they don't know won't hurt me." She asked the man to hold them, and they moved down the aisle. She had no intention of using the cookbooks. Chances were, they'd stay in the back of her car until she could donate them to a charity.

"I want to taste the first thing you cook. Rob can be your guinea pig too."

Danielle stopped to look at her friend. "Do you have a death wish? Besides, I thought you liked your husband."

"I do, but to keep you honest, I'll be your first taste tester. And you're not allowed to leave the books in the back of your SUV or give them away. Try your new hobby." With that, Trish raced to another table and picked up a chinoiserie bowl.

When she caught up with her friend, Danielle said, "You already have one like that."

"I did." She shrugged. "But you know ... there are so many surfaces."

"That's why you needed that lamp." Danielle's jaw dropped. "Come to think of it, that entry table is new too. You two are disgusting."

"You're jealous."

She sucked in a breath and let out a sigh. "You're right." She moved through the rows. "Is it really that good?"

"What? The sex?" Trish turned and headed down the next aisle. "Remember that better-than-sex, chocolate cake Ms. Ferguson made?"

Danielle gasped. "No. Better than that?" That cake was an orgasm without a man.

"It's ten times that."

She shouldered her friend. "I would hate you if I didn't love you so much." Trish was the sister she always wanted, but not one of the two she had by blood. They met their freshman year of college and were inseparable. Trish's family was much like her own, except Danielle's father never wore a yarmulke and he ate bacon and pork ribs like they were the only meat in the world.

"And because you love me, you'll keep an open mind when I tell you what I did?" Trish led her to the funnel cake booth and ordered two with extra sugar.

"If it needs extra sugar, then it's got to be bad." She clenched her jaw until her teeth hurt. "What did you do?"

Trish picked up a funnel cake and stepped back. "It's not *that* bad."

"If you're buying sweets, it's bad. You also gave yourself running room, which means it's worse than bad. Spill it."

Trish stepped back once more. "I worked it out so you have an appointment with Aunt Freida."

Danielle's mind raced through Trish's relatives until she figured out who Freida was.

"You did not." She took a large bite of the sugary cake trying to cover the bitter taste in her mouth. "Aunt Freida, the matchmaker?"

"Yes, she set up my parents and my sister and my brother. She has a sixty percent success rate with women on the shelf."

Danielle choked, and a puff of sugar floated around them. "I'm not on the shelf. I'm only thirty-five."

Trish smiled. "My point exactly."

"Hey, you just promised no more set-ups if I agreed to try a hobby."

"No, I said no more trolls. Aunt Freida's got stellar taste. She'll find you a good man." With a flick of her finger, Trish removed the excess sugar from her plate, and they were once again surrounded by a sweet cloud. "She's expecting you tomorrow at noon. I'll text you her address. Keep in mind, she never works on Sunday, but you're family."

"No, no, no, I can't have your family setting me up. I'm not ..."

Trish lifted her perfectly plucked brow. "Jewish?"

"No. You know race, religion, and status mean nothing to me. I want to find love organically. It shouldn't be a business deal."

Trish let out a huff. "With a marriage failure rate of fifty percent, why wouldn't you enter it like a business deal?"

"Did you and Rob enter matrimony with an outlined contract?"

"Yes, but it was verbal. I told him if he ever made me unhappy, I'd kill him." She cocked her head and grinned.

"I can show you some episodes of *Murder, She Wrote* that might come in handy. As long as Angela Lansbury doesn't show up, you should be fine."

They walked the rest of the way through the market. Trish bought everything to do with baking. There were measuring spoons and cups, and an apron that said, *spooning leads to forking.*

She handed them to Danielle. "I'm supporting your new hobby."

Danielle suppressed a groan. Now she'd have to pull out a cookbook and attempt to make something that wouldn't kill them all.

"I'll invite you over for a scheduled poisoning soon."

They picked up their purchases and headed to the car. When they got back to Trish's house, she leaned over and gave Danielle a hug. "You're worthy of more than you got. Never forget that. There is a man looking for you."

"Should I hoist a flag that says, 'I'm over here?'"

"No, but don't be late to Aunt Freida's, or she might curse you instead of blessing you."

"I don't want to go. What if she says I'm hopeless?"

Trish gathered her purchases and climbed out of the SUV. "I'll help you buy some cats."

Chapter 2

JAMES

James Parks walked inside the temporary Aspen headquarters of Luxe Resorts. He didn't wear a custom-made suit or a pair of Italian loafers like he usually did during takeovers or meetings. Today, he wore jeans and a T-shirt. While he felt comfortable in both, he preferred the laid-back feel of denim and cotton.

"Mr. Parks." The front desk security guard nodded.

"Good morning, Tony. Did Allie and Julian arrive?" On a lark, he, his sister, and his best friend started Luxe resorts ten years ago. They set out to prove that everyone could afford luxury.

"Julian is in the conference room, and your sister called and said she's picking up breakfast for you heathens."

"Heathens, huh?"

Tony's shoulders shook with laughter. "Her words, not mine."

"I got ya." He tapped the counter and moved toward the elevator. "Have a great day, Tony."

"You too, sir."

Arriving on the top floor, he went straight to the conference room where Julian was fussing with the coffeemaker.

"Just give up already."

"One day, I will master this." Julian looked at the items in his hands.

"It's not rocket science." James took the coffee pouch, strainer, and pot from his friend. "It's kind of like making love. You put all the pieces in the proper places, and the outcome is amazing." He put the pot on the burner, tucked the pouch inside the strainer, and slid it all home. He pressed the button to start, and in seconds, the smell of heaven filled the air.

They leaned on the counter and waited for the pot to finish the brew cycle. "Are you glad to be back in Aspen?" Julian asked.

He wasn't from Colorado. Julian was New York-born and raised. They'd met at Cornell. Julian had studied economics, while James' focus was architecture.

"I love it here. Now, if I can find the time to get my own place."

Julian rolled his eyes. "I can give you the name of the woman I used." He waggled his brows. "She does a thorough job at showcasing the amenities."

"You're such a gigolo."

"Yes, I am, but at least I have a home, and I'm not bunking with my sister at my father's place."

"I'm not sharing a room with Allie. That's just gross. She has the west wing of the house. I have the east."

"Remember the parties we had at college. I miss those," Julian sighed.

"Grow up, man, you're racing toward forty. Can't be Peter Pan your whole life."

"I'm thirty-six, and I can try."

"I brought bagels," Allie said as she entered.

"Epstein's or Abrams'?" James always believed quality was in the ingredients, and while Epstein's put out a good product, nothing beat a bagel with a long family history. The Abrams arrived in Aspen from New York decades ago, bringing with them the best bagels in the country.

She huffed. "Abrams, of course." She turned to James. "I got that disgusting veggie cream cheese you like."

"What about the honey spread for me?" Julian asked.

"I always take care of you because you can't take care of yourself."

Julian laughed. "I can, but I don't have to when you do everything for me."

She set the box on the table. "Pour me a cup, and let's get started. You two are wasting my Saturday."

James knew that wasn't the truth. Allie did nothing on the weekends but binge-watch television and crochet. He had a two-foot stack of unused afghans next to his sofa. When he asked her why she insisted on crocheting so many, she told him it kept her hands out of the cookie jar.

"Is everything signed?" he asked. Julian was the numbers and contracts guy.

"We're good to go." He slid a folder to each one of them. "Open to page one, and let's go over the details."

During the next two hours, they talked about the different phases to bring their newest acquisition into the Luxe family. This was the tenth property they had acquired. They'd opened one a year since they'd gone into business together. This would be the last for a while. Moving from location to location was exhausting. He and Allie had come full circle and were back to the place they'd once called home. As for Julian ... he was happy wherever there were women.

"Are you staying under the radar again?" Allie asked. She smeared a bagel with plain cream cheese.

"No, I'm blending in. Working the construction side of the business allows me anonymity." He rose and headed for the coffee pot, which was almost empty. "You know I love the building and remodeling part, and I like to mingle with the people. Being inconspicuous allows me to see how things run." He plopped back into his chair. "When I arrive in jeans and steel-toed boots, people don't feel threatened. If someone asked point-blank if I was an owner, I'd tell them exactly who I am, but they never do." He pointed from Allie to Julian. "When you two arrive looking straight out of the boardroom, people stop talking."

"Not true. Everyone talks to me." Allie took a bite of her bagel and set the rest aside.

"'Where did you get those shoes', doesn't count."

"It does if I'm in the gift shop." She pulled out the last sheet of paper and scanned it with squinting eyes. "Let's go over the management."

Julian took his pen and starred a few names on his page. "After looking through the financials, I have concerns about a few people."

"Let's start at the top. What about the general manager, Avis Barber?" James asked.

"Gone," Allie answered.

"That bad?" He brought his half-filled cup to his lips.

"We didn't fire her, she quit." Allie lifted a sheet of paper into the air. "This was in my email inbox at the close of business yesterday."

Julian crossed her name off his list. "Good. One less worry. Besides, she wasn't overseeing her departments well. Outdoor recreation has been running at a deficit for years. That should be a place where we're making a killing. With the equipment paid for, the only expense should be upkeep and labor." He circled that department on his page. "Food and beverage are the same. They aren't efficient."

James looked at the names. "What about Danielle Morgan? She's in charge of guest relations."

Julian leaned back in his chair. "Feedback on her is good, although reservations are down. It might be best if we replace all the management and start fresh."

"Let's see what we're dealing with before we swing the ax." James rummaged through the pile of pages to find the financials for her department. "A decrease in reservations can be a symptom of many things, like poor upper management, the condition of the property, and the increase in resorts fees."

They'd spent months in negotiations with Atlas Properties for this location. The old company had invested little in the infrastructure over the years, and it showed in dwindling revenue, which was a blessing for Luxe because they'd wanted to get their hands on a property in or near Aspen for years. Timberline was a sleeper community and the perfect location for an all-inclusive resort.

"How long will it take to get our new offices built?"

"Once I evaluate the space, I should have them finished within thirty days. We can move our offices over to the resort and let go of the rented space in this building." They didn't need to consolidate. They were hugely profitable with their business model, but they didn't believe in waste either. With properties in Vail, Breckenridge, San Diego, San Francisco, New York, Miami, London, Paris and Beijing, they were bringing all-inclusive to the world. They hoped to nab a property in Sydney, one in Morocco, maybe one in St Petersburg someday. The options were limitless. "Can we bring Tony with us? I'll miss his smiling face."

Allie laughed. "Do you have a man-crush?"

"Nope, but I think he's a good guy and a hard worker." He thought about Tony's five kids, and Joleen, his wife for over a decade. "Just thinking about people who commit to their jobs. I respect Tony for the work he's done in this building. He always has a smile, and he's willing to go above and beyond."

"You're right." She jotted his name on the top of the page. "Let's find him a job."

"If that's all we have to go over, I'm heading to the site to get a sneak peek before all hell breaks loose on Monday."

"You'll be here for the management meeting, right?"

He nodded toward the adjoining room. The one behind the mirror they used for opinion polls. "I'll sit in, but incognito." He patted the conference table. "You know this isn't my thing. You two be the brains, and I'll be the brawn."

Julian smiled. "You want us to keep you out of the press release?"

James shook his head. "Nah, release under my legal name. No one knows that I'm Alistair Parks Jr." His father owned the naming disasters in the family. Since their mother's name was Allison, he thought it would be good to stick with A names. With a sister named Allie, and a dog named Alimony, he'd rebelled and went by his middle name, James.

He stood and moved toward the door. "You know where to find me."

WALKING into a new property was like drinking a double shot latte. Energy coursed through his veins as if he'd mainlined his caffeine that morning. There was so much that needed fixing in this location, including getting rid of the giant fake floral arrangement that blocked the view of the lobby. It was as good as a stop sign.

He pulled his keycard from his pocket and entered the last elevator on the right. It was the only one that reached the executive offices. The doors opened to a darkened hallway. The hum of computer fans filled the air. That and the scent of fresh-brewed coffee.

He lifted his nose and followed the smell. Confetti colored carpet ate up the noise of his steel-toed boots. The smell of dark roast carried him down the hallway like the fluff of a dandelion caught on a breeze.

He turned into the only lighted space and leaned on the door-jamb. All he could see was the backside of a woman. Those curves could never belong to a man. She poured herself a cup of coffee and then waterfalled sugar into her mug.

"There are easier ways to die than a diabetic coma."

She dropped the sugar container, which landed on the edge of her cup, catapulting it into the air and all over her shirt.

She hopped back, but there was no escaping the heat that bled into the pink cotton. "Holy hell." She pulled the material away from her skin. "Who are you?" She reached for the paper towels at the same time he did, their hands colliding midair.

He pulled out several and pressed them against the stain. "I'm so sorry to scare you."

She swiped them from his hand and began blotting the mess.

"This is a total loss." She huffed out a sigh. "I loved this shirt."

With her head down, he hadn't seen her face, but as she lifted her eyes to meet his, he saw they were the most beautiful hazel. Not blue and green hazel, but brown and green with a ring the color of the sun at the center.

"I'm sorry for your loss. Should we have a funeral service?"

"A comedian, huh?" She stared at him. "Who are you?"

He crumbled the towels she'd placed on the counter and tossed them into the trash. "I'm James."

"Tell me, James, what are you doing here?"

"Outside of ruining your shirt?" He stared at how the cotton sucked against her skin. How every peak and valley of her upper body showed. "I'm ... checking things out."

"Do you have a reason to be in the executive offices on a Saturday afternoon?"

"I do. Do you?"

"I'm Danielle Morgan. Manager of guest relations."

Ah, the woman they'd discussed briefly not too long ago. Her job also included concierge services, the front desk, and reservations. He would expect to find her here Monday through Friday, but not on the weekend.

"Do you normally work weekends?"

"I practically live here, but that doesn't explain your presence." She looked past him to the phone. "Should I worry? Do I need to call security?"

He pulled out his keycard and employee identification card, which he flashed at her quickly, then tucked them back into his pocket. "I'm allowed. I came here to look at the offices. We'll be reconfiguring the workspace starting next week. Figured it would be good to get a lay of the land first."

"We?" It was his first day, and he'd already blown his cover.

When he said we, he fully meant Allie, Julian, and himself, but she didn't know that.

"My crew. We're starting work on Monday."

"So, you're the one hired by the new owners."

"I am. Would you care to show me around?"

She glanced down at her T-shirt, which left little to the imagination. "Give me a minute to change, and I'll be glad to give you the ten-cent tour." She scurried from the break area.

While he waited, he poured himself a cup of coffee and took in the space. It was awful. Chipped Formica counters held a stained plastic coffee maker and a microwave that was at least ten years old. The amenities for the employees were dismal. They weren't much better for the guests.

She raced back, tucking a white blouse into her jeans. "Sorry about that." She picked up her coffee and led him down the hallway. "You've seen the break area." She turned a corner into a large room divided into cubicles. "These are the management offices."

"You mean cubicles."

"That's what they are. However, that's not what we're trained to call them. You know ... appearances and all." She set her cup on a tidy desk labeled with her name. "This is where the other department heads and I work." She looked over her shoulder. "That office belongs to the general manager, Avis."

"She's gone," he blurted without thought.

Her hand went to her mouth. "Oh my, did they fire her?" Her eyes grew big. "She's not dead, is she?"

He was exchanging information that, in reality, he shouldn't have known if he was merely a construction lead.

"No idea," he said. "They told me to start at this end and work my way down. I assumed she left."

He walked into the enormous office and looked around. Why the general manager needed this kind of space was beyond him. Realigned, he could repurpose the square footage for several offices. He pointed to a door at the back of the room.

"Where does that lead to?"

She shrugged. "I'm not exactly sure, but rumor has it there's an apartment hidden behind that door."

"A what? Avis needed an apartment?"

"I think it was there from when the original owners of the resort lived on site. Then when it sold to Atlas Inc., there was a rumor the CEO kept his mistress there. I think there's an elevator that goes to the garage. Avis never entered through the common area. She seemed to teleport, so I figure at least part of the rumor was true."

"That's just insane. Why have an apartment when there's an entire hotel at your disposal?"

She lifted her shoulders. "I couldn't say."

Several long strides and he was at the door. When he swung it open, he was surrounded in luxury. He'd been in the resort's guestrooms. He'd even visited the suites. None of them were decorated as tastefully as this. The floors were marble. The draperies silk. The furnishings custom.

"Wow." Danielle moved through the living area to the kitchen and touched the espresso machine. "No wonder Avis didn't spend time in the break room."

"I'm surprised anyone does. More surprised that, as the guest relations and reservation manager, you'd be clueless about this space. Shouldn't you know everything about this hotel?"

Her jaw dropped open. "For your information Mr. ..." She stared at his chest as if looking for his name tag.

"James, just James." He leaned against the wall and watched the fuse he lit burn.

Her outrage showed in the flames spreading from her chest to her cheeks. He could tell a lot about a person by the way they filtered their anger. What would the lovely Ms. Morgan do?

"Okay, Mr. Just James. I'm very good at what I do. There are several areas of this hotel I've not been in, like the boiler room. You know why?"

A smile pulled at the corners of his lips. "No, tell me."

"Because I can't rent the space out. I don't hang out in the garage, the ski equipment rentals, or the kitchen. There are managers in charge of those departments." She swirled her hand in the air. "This is not a room I can rent, so it's irrelevant to me."

"Half the resort is vacant." He wanted to bite his tongue. It was more information he shouldn't have had.

"How would you know?"

"I'll be remodeling the rooms. So much easier to remove an outdated bathtub when someone's not soaking in it."

"Mr. James."

"Just James."

She huffed. "This is a large resort with many areas that need improvement. We are entering off-season. I can only speak to the area I'm responsible for, but I'm a damn sorcerer with managing reservations. I run a five-star resort on a motel budget. What do you know about running a resort?"

"I know that this one is outdated and wouldn't have sold if it was profitable."

"And somehow that's my fault?"

"It's everyone's fault. A business is like a relationship. If it's nourished and cared for, it thrives. Otherwise, it fails." He turned and walked out of the apartment. "I'll see you Monday morning."

"Thanks for the warning."

As he entered the elevator, he laughed. Danielle Morgan entertained him, and it had been a long time since a woman made him feel anything but agitation.

Chapter 3

DANIELLE

"Damn man kept me awake all night long." Danielle rushed around the house, gathering her purse and giving herself a final look in the mirror. She brushed at the dark circles under her eyes and growled. How was it a man she'd just met could enter her dreams? Dreams that made her toss and turn and heat the entire night.

Her phone rang. Expecting it to be Trish, she answered, "I'm on my way. I promised I wouldn't be late, and I won't." She rushed out the door to her SUV. As she rounded the back, she thought about the books she'd bought yesterday.

"Most people start a conversation with hello." His was a voice she recognized and loathed.

"What do you want, Chris?"

He chuckled. "I'd love to know where you're going. Got a date?"

"None of your business." She'd never tell him she was meeting a matchmaker. There would be no end to the jeering she'd receive if he knew. "Why did you call?"

"Did you get the email?"

She climbed into the driver's side and started the engine. If she didn't get moving, she'd definitely be late.

"What email?"

"From Luxe? You know the company that recently took over, or have you been living under a rock?"

As she backed out of her driveway, someone laid on their horn and swerved to miss her. "You're distracting me. I almost got hit."

"I take it that's a no."

She pulled onto the road and headed toward Aspen, where Trish's Aunt Freida lived. If she was lucky, she'd make it with a few seconds to spare.

"I haven't read it. What does it say?"

"Mandatory meeting for department heads at Luxe Resorts offices in Aspen tomorrow at ten."

The words rolled around in her brain. A mandatory meeting couldn't be good. "Supposedly, Avis left." It was no longer a rumor in her mind. She'd been in the office and saw that all the ceramic clowns Avis collected were no longer on the shelves. It was as if she'd never been there.

"Shit. You think they'll fire us all?"

"Doubt it. I'm sure they'll look at each of us individually." It was a jab toward him because his record would never stand on its own. Now she knew why he called. "You're afraid I'll throw you under the bus to save my ass, aren't you?"

Silence filled the inside of the car. The only sound was the thunk of her tires moving over uneven asphalt.

"I hoped that you'd have my back like you did last time."

"I won't tell them you bang the guests in their rooms if that's what you mean, but I won't lie to them if they ask."

"So, you won't tell them about Margie?"

She laughed. "You mean Margie, Laurie, Stella, and Angie?" She turned onto Freida's street. "Nope, that's not my business. Not my stories to tell, and you're not mine to protect. I've got to go."

"Where are you?"

"You're no longer entitled to information about my private life."

She would have loved to tell him she was on a date, but she didn't like to lie.

"I'll see you Monday," he said.

"Thanks for the warning." She hung up and cussed at him the rest of the way. She didn't normally swear, but Chris brought out the absolute worst in her. She let out expletives that could make a sailor blush.

Now pushing the time, she climbed out of the car and raced up the sidewalk. With each step, she tried to forget that she'd been driven batshit crazy by two annoying men in as many days. Maybe Freida could tilt the scales for her.

She stood on the welcome mat, took a deep breath, and replaced her frown with a smile. As she raised her hand to knock, the door opened.

"You're late." Freida was a sight to see with her black hair and white sweep of bangs. She looked Danielle up and down like she was a stray. "And you're a mess." She stood aside for her to enter.

She should have realized from the outside that the house would be over the top inside as well. She had rushed past hedges trimmed to look like animals and flowerbeds that had a June bloomed look in April.

"Sorry, there was traffic."

Freida lifted a jet-black brow. "On a Sunday?"

"Church services and garage sale seekers." She stood on the marble flooring and visually followed the spiral staircase to rest her eyes on a big portrait of Freida and her husband taking up the entire wall of the landing above.

"Peter Rosenberg painted that picture," Freida said with pride.

Danielle didn't know who that was, but if Freida paid more than a nickel for that portrait, it was too much. "It's lovely." She hated to lie, but sometimes it was necessary. There was no way she'd tell Freida that the head of the fox on her fur stole appeared ready to bite her jugular. Her husband leaned so far away from her she feared he'd fall off the canvas.

"Follow me. We have so much work to do and so little time. Every second that passes makes you less desirable."

She wanted to take offense, but the woman was a matchmaker with a sixty percent success rate. That was better than her one hundred percent failure rate. How could she argue?

Freida led them into a living room decorated in white and gold. She pointed to the sofa, but Danielle was afraid to sit on the pristine white fabric. Instead, she took a seat on the gold silk footstool.

"Doesn't follow directions," Freida said and jotted down something on a piece of paper laid out on the grand piano.

"That's not true."

"Argumentative."

Danielle opened her mouth to say something, and Freida made a zip motion across her lips.

Danielle's mouth snapped shut.

"Stand up."

She did as Freida asked and waited for her to complain about her black slacks, her silver blouse, and her hair that needed a cut.

"You have good posture."

That came as a surprise. "Thank you."

"But that's about it." Freida touched Danielle's hair. "You need a cut, but the color is lovely. It's like a high-end whiskey. And your eyes, they are interesting. Like a green meadow during a landslide."

She wasn't sure if that was a compliment or a put-down. "Thank you?"

"Since we can't turn back the clock, we have to find other selling points. Do you have money saved?"

"I'm comfortable."

Freida's eyes lit up. "That's wonderful. Are you six-figure or seven-figure comfortable?" She tapped her pen on the paper. "Eight?"

The embarrassment tasted like dirt and lodged like a boulder in her throat. "I'm four-figure comfortable." She would not mention that her savings were low four figures. It had only been a year since she finalized her divorce, and she'd spent the entire time paying down the debts Chris had accrued on her credit cards. It was her fault she let him transfer his debt under the guise of consolidating.

"Destitute." Freida scribbled on the paper. "What about assets? Do you have stocks or bonds?"

That good posture commented on earlier appeared to sag when the weight of her shoulders rolled forward.

"I have a house?"

"In Aspen?"

She shook her head. "Timberline."

Freida scribbled something else on the paper.

"What did you write?" Danielle swiped the page from the piano. The last entry was "Hopeless." She pulled out her phone.

"Who are you calling?"

Freida sat on the sofa. Her black skirt hugged her legs as she swept them to the side. If Danielle had to describe the woman, she'd say she was a cross between Cruella de Vil with her black and white hair, and Joan Collins with her attitude and fashion sense.

"I'm calling your niece to tell her to bring over the cats."

Freida leaned forward and covered the phone. "Don't fret. I'm not a quitter. I had a caliber of man in mind, but lowering our expectations could open the window to love."

"How far do we need to lower the bar?" Was she talking about going from dating a rich man to seeing a blue-collar worker? At that thought, a vision of James floated through her brain. Jeans that hugged strong thighs. A T-shirt that stretched across broad shoulders and tapered down to the washboard abs she knew were hiding beneath the cotton. She perked up. "I have no problem with a working man."

Freida laughed. "Oh honey, we'll be lucky to find any man to take you on. You're past prime birthing. You're attractive in a girl-next-door way, but this is Aspen. Unless you're willing to nip, tuck, and fill, we have to be realistic. A rich man? That's like putting nothing on a hook and hoping to catch a marlin."

"So now I'm a worm?"

Freida shook her head. "No sweetheart, you're the hook." She rose from her seat. "I have one option. He's a nice man. He's got a good job. I think he'd be happy with a project like you."

"Is he Jewish?"

"Yes."

"And that won't be a problem because I'm not?"

Freida laughed. "You can convert, lots of people do. There's Sammy Davis Junior, Isla Fisher, and Tom Arnold."

"Who is this guy?" She turned and twisted the fabric of her pants.

"His name is Gene Horowitz."

Danielle nearly fell off the stool. "No way." She popped up, grabbed her bag, and headed toward the door.

"Where are you going?"

"To the store. I'll need litter and cat food. Thanks for everything Freida, but I fear you might be right. I am hopeless."

She'd had reached her car when her phone rang. This time she knew it was Trish.

"You owe me," Danielle said as she climbed inside. She took off so quickly she could hear the box in the back shift.

"I heard. I'm sorry."

"You should be. This was worse than having a waxing. Your aunt stripped me of my confidence and self-esteem."

"She can be harsh, but she's got a—"

"I know, a sixty percent success ratio. She's also got horrible taste in furniture and art."

Trish laughed. "You saw the Peter Rosenberg?"

"Hard to miss. It's like looking at a six-inch pimple on a two-inch nose. Impossible."

"What will you do now?"

"I'm going to the store to buy a gallon of birthday cake ice cream, and then I'm heading home to watch episodes of *Murder, She Wrote* to see if there's a way I can kill you and get away with it."

"But it isn't your birthday."

Leave it to Trish to skate over the murder plot and go straight to the ice cream. She knew Danielle only ate birthday cake flavor on her special day. In her opinion, a gallon of ice cream was a good starting point to sweeten her sour mood.

"I'm starting over, a rebirth if you will."

"That's my girl, and while you're there, pick up whatever you need to bake with because I told you I'd be your first victim."

"I don't think they sell arsenic at Safeway." She hung up and went home because there was already a gallon of chocolate peanut butter cup in the freezer.

Once her car pulled to a stop in the drive, she got out and walked to the back. The books were still in the box, but one caught her attention. She hadn't noticed it when she purchased the box and wondered if the vendor had added it after she paid. It was a tattered, well-worn book with a big heart on the cover. In bold black print was, **Recipes for Love-Unlock Your Heart's Desire.** In smaller letters on the bottom were the words, **For your eyes only**.

She opened the hatch and pulled it out. There was something intriguing about secrets.

DANIELLE BRUSHED past the cookbook on her counter to the coffee pot. Once she'd gotten home yesterday afternoon, she wasn't in the mood to look at recipes for love, especially since she was a recipe for disaster.

She poured a cup of coffee and added in her usual heavy-handed helping of sugar. She picked up the folder she'd spent all night assembling. It was a mini dossier of her department and their accomplishments. If she was one thing, she was prepared. She'd learned early on to have what her bosses wanted before they knew they wanted it. She hoped the new owners of the resort found value in her professionalism.

If she left now, she'd arrive at least twenty minutes early which was basically her idea of being on time.

It wasn't that she agreed with the adage that the early bird got the worm. In her mind, the early bird kept her job, and that was her top priority.

Her insides crawled with nerves as she climbed behind the steering wheel. Was Chris right? Would they fire them all and start fresh with a new team?

Halfway to the meeting, she glanced down at the folder on her passenger seat. A horn blared, and when she looked up, a yellow lab was cowering in the center of her lane. She slammed on the breaks and attempted to steer clear of the dog, but with cars on both sides, there was nowhere to go. She held her breath and waited for the sound of impact as she screeched to a stop, but she heard nothing.

After a quick once over to make sure she was in one piece, she jumped out to make sure the dog wasn't injured, but when she rounded the SUV, the dog was gone.

"Thank God," she said out loud. It was a blessing that she hadn't hit the dog. Outside of not being able to live with herself if she had, the whole ordeal would have made her late. She climbed back inside, took a deep breath and picked up her coffee to take a sip. Just as the cup touched her lips, a jarring crunch sent her SUV lurching forward and her coffee toppling down the front of her shirt. In her rearview mirror, she could see the flailing arms of the angry man who had hit her. "You've got to be kidding me?"

Chapter 4

JAMES

The two-way mirror once drove James crazy, but now it served a purpose. As the department heads filed into the conference room, he sat behind the mirror and took notes.

First impressions were important. He figured an invitation to the cooperate offices meant business, and he expected people to be in uniform or dressed to impress.

Sitting on the desk in front of him were the employee files with their pictures clipped to the front.

The head of security walked in first. His name tag was chipped, and James could barely make out the name Paul Bradley.

James wrote his first impressions.

Uniform is too small. Buttons ready to burst.

Big man—order for his size.

Wrinkled and stained—sloppy.

It didn't matter because no one was staying in their current uniforms. Luxe had its own look and ready-to-break-free bellies weren't in the brand. They'd custom make a shirt for Paul if necessary.

Next was Willetta Frost. Housekeeping had good reviews, and she was being considered for advancement.

Pressed uniform.

Put together.

The door opened and in walked Flynn McHale who apologized profusely for being a few minutes late. He said he liked to oversee all produce deliveries and today's order got delayed.

Clean uniform.

Neat appearance.

Flustered.

Product quality conscious.

James put a star on the corner of his employee file. Running at a deficit in food and beverage wasn't unusual. Food was always a loss in resorts, and when this one went all-inclusive, keeping food costs down would be important, but keeping customers' satisfaction up was key. Flynn McHale might be a candidate for general manager.

He turned to the man arriving with Flynn. This guy had to be Chris Putnam and he delivered a good first impression.

Khaki shorts.

Polo shirt.

Boat shoes.

Hair neatly trimmed.

Dressed appropriately for his outdoor recreation department.

He glanced around the table once more and found that the department head for guest services was still missing. He was generally good at reading people, and Danielle didn't seem like the type to be late.

His sister Allie arrived wearing some kind of designer suit. It was a soft pink to put people at ease. She was good with people and never put them in a defensive position at the first meeting. She only brought the black suit out for serious situations, like firings and takeovers. She referred to it as her Gucci guillotine. Allie was a force of nature.

"Good morning, everyone. Welcome to the Luxe family. This is the tenth property under the Luxe name. We apologize for not meeting you sooner. When the property became available, we had to move quickly. Our lawyer Michael Stratton brokered the deal while we tied up loose ends at our last location." She pointed to the table where name tags sat in front of each chair. "Find your seat, and let's get started. Future meetings will take place at our offices at the resort."

"You're moving to the offices?" Willetta asked.

"Yes, it makes sense to be on the property," Allie answered.

The door opened and Danielle nearly fell into the room looking flustered and disheveled. Pulled tightly to her chest like an armor breastplate was a folder. The kind that opened to show three brass tacks down the middle and a pocket to each side.

"Way to impress," Chris said. "Glad you could make it." He glanced at the clock on the wall. "You're only ten minutes late."

"I'm so sorry." Her head shook back and forth. Tiny strands of brown hair escaped the tight bun at the nape of her neck. "I had a fender bender ..." She let out a whoosh of air. "I apologize for being late." She took the empty seat next to Chris. He whispered something to her, and she gave him a hard glare and turned away.

James wrote down his first impressions.

Hot

After crossing out that word, he began again.

Frazzled.

Late.

Nervous.

Did she think she was losing her job? They never cleaned house on the first day. Everyone from vendors to employees deserved a chance to prove their worth.

The Pines Resort was a mess when they made the deal. Buying the place was a huge risk given they'd be upside down for several years, but the forecast showed that once they converted it into a Luxe property, they would quickly make up the deficit. Anything with value was worth the investment, whether money, time, patience, or people.

Allie looked toward the mirror as if she were saying "Are you getting all of this?"

She cleared her throat. "As I was saying, welcome to the Luxe family. As a family, we are all on a first name basis. I'm Allie, your Chief Operations Officer and the person now in charge of Human Resources." She pointed to the name tags on the table. "If you will be kind enough to grab your new badges and put them on, it will help me remember who you are." She picked up Todd Lundgren's name tag. "Engineering won't be present because of a problem at the resort. Something about a water leak in the basement."

"That would be boiler number one," Danielle said. "It's been a problem for years." She continued to hug the folder to her chest.

James knew his sister. She was smiling, but she was a savvy businesswoman. She watched everything and was taking mental notes.

The first to comply was Danielle. She picked her tag up and pinned it perfectly straight to her lapel without losing her shield. The other's haphazardly put theirs on. All but Chris. He didn't budge.

Allie walked around the table and picked his up. "Hi Chris," She placed the tag in his hand. "Put this on, so I don't forget you."

"Oh darlin', I'm unforgettable. You won't need a nameplate to remember me."

Her heels clicked on the tile floor as she went back to the head of the table. "You're right. I'll make a note that you're the one who can't follow directions."

A knock sounded, the door opened, and Julian stepped inside carrying a travel container from Pikes Perk, and a box of pastries.

"Did I miss anything?" He placed the items in the middle of the conference table and told everyone to help themselves. Food had a way of putting people at ease.

"Just introductions," Allie said.

"I'm Julian. I'm the Chief Financial Officer."

Chris held up his name tag. "I'm Chris." He opened the box and touched several pastries before he settled on the cherry danish.

Paul was next, followed by Flynn, and then Willetta. Danielle passed.

"Just coffee for me, please. I've eaten already." She reached one hand out for a cup and filled it, then looked around the table as if searching for something. "Do you have sugar?"

Julian pulled a few packets out of his pocket and set them down.

She stared at them for several seconds before taking one. Somehow, she managed to keep the folder in place while she emptied the sugar into her cup. Her whole body shuddered at the first sip.

Danielle was fascinating to watch. He chuckled but covered his mouth. He'd seen her put sugar into her cup, and she was more of an I'll have some coffee with my sugar type of woman.

"Let's get started," Allie said.

Julian took a seat to Allie's right and waited.

"First, I'd like to announce that Avis is no longer with the company."

A collective gasp filled the air, and heads turned from side to side as if the answer for her absence was written on a nearby face. Danielle sat up straight and nursed her coffee. A twitch of her lip followed each drink.

Willetta piped in, "Did you can her lazy ass?"

James crossed out her name as a candidate for promotion. Avis might have been lazy, but there was no reason for Willetta's disparaging remarks. An excellent general manager needed to filter their words. She didn't appear to have one.

Julian sat tall. "We won't be discussing other's employment records, but we will talk about the financial health of your departments."

There wasn't a sound. Not a breath in or an exhale out.

"We brought you here so we can answer your questions and tell you about the future of The Pines, now Luxe Resort at Timberline."

Flynn raised his hand, which was polite, but it reminded James of his days in elementary school. "How long will we be here?"

Chris piped in. "Yes, how long?"

Allie's brows lifted. "You two have a date? Maybe together?"

Chris smiled warmly. "I've got inventory to do. It's important to keep things organized."

James didn't miss the look of disbelief he saw on several faces.

Danielle tightened her grip on the folder. "Maybe if we stopped interrupting Allie, everything would move more quickly. I, for one, would love to know the company's plans for the resort and for us."

Allie walked over to an easel and presented the concept. She flipped page after page to show the vision for the all-inclusive property. They would vacate the building by floors and wings for remodeling. The cabins by the lake would get renovated last since they were booked solid through the summer.

When she finished, she opened the floor for questions.

Danielle looked down at her folder several times.

Curious about its contents, James texted his sister.

Her phone lit up, and she quickly read the message.

What's Danielle got in front of her?

Paul from security sat as far forward as his stomach allowed. The man was like the tower in Pisa, Italy, cocked to the side.

"Aren't there three of you?" Paul asked.

Allie looked toward the mirror James sat behind. "Yes, my brother Alistair is the Chief Executive Officer."

"Will we meet him?" Danielle asked.

"He's overseeing a project. He likes to remain in the background, but he'll be around." Allie looked down at the folder. "Did you have something you wanted to share, Danielle?"

Danielle took in a big breath and closed her eyes before she lowered the folder to the table. In the process, she exposed a white blouse covered with coffee.

James laughed out loud, though no one could hear him. "That

32

looks familiar." He had a flashback to the wet T-shirt he'd encountered in the lounge two days before.

She pushed her coffee to the side and opened her folder. "I wasn't sure what type of meeting this would be, so I put together some profit-and-loss reports for my department. I also jotted down ideas for improving the customer experience."

Chris coughed, and James thought he heard him say, "suck up", but couldn't be certain.

Allie reached out to take the reports. "Thank you, Danielle. That shows initiative." She eyed her soiled blouse and in turn, Danielle turned crimson.

"I don't normally ... never mind. This is unacceptable, and it won't happen again."

Allie nodded and scanned the top page. "You dislike the fake flowers in the lobby too?"

James fist bumped the air and put a star on her folder for having taste.

"I'm not a fan of fake." She looked around the table and stopped at Chris. "Our guests deserve better."

"I agree." Allie tucked the pages into her briefcase and closed it. "One more thing. With Avis gone, we'll be looking to fill her position. As department heads, we hope to advance one of your careers."

Julian stood up. "I'll need reports from all of you by the end of next week outlining your successes and ideas for improvements." He walked to the door and stopped. "I'll also need your quarterly expense reports." He exited, followed by Allie. The click-clack of her heels fading with each step.

James waited in the room to see what would happen next.

Willetta laughed and said she'd be happy to get a raise.

Chris opened the box and took out another pastry. "I'll fight you for it."

Paul struggled to stand. When he gained his balance, he shuffled out of the room, grumbling about the homework.

Flynn waved to everyone and left.

Only Danielle remained. She looked at the mess and cleaned up the table. She set the coffee neatly in the center and covered the left-over pastries. On her way out, she walked to the mirror and looked at her refection. She rubbed under her eyes as if she could erase the dark circles.

He wondered what had caused them.

They were so close James could almost smell her perfume; almost feel her breath against his cheek.

"What are you thinking, Danielle?"

She tugged at her soiled shirt and answered the question she couldn't have heard.

"It's too early to drink and too late to run."

Chapter 5

DANIELLE

"Danielle." Liz, from the front desk, waved her over. She was glad she took the time to stop at home to change her shirt because she set the example for her staff.

She had hoped to skate through the lobby and make her way to the thirteenth floor where the executive offices were. She wasn't superstitious, but now the thirteenth floor seemed foreboding. They were under new ownership, and that would change things. She feared it would change everything. If their first impressions of her were what she thought they'd been, she'd be lucky if her final check wasn't already waiting for her on her desk.

She put on her weekday smile. "Hey Liz, what can I do for you?"

"Is it true that Avis is no longer with us?"

Danielle laughed. "You make it sound like she died. As far as I know, she's still around, but she won't be working for Luxe."

"Wow, they fired her?"

"I don't know the details." She considered Julian's statement about not discussing employment records. "All I know is we will need to adjust and adapt to the new management."

Liz slapped the granite counter. It was the only nice thing about the lobby. "I hate change."

Danielle had experienced a lot of change lately. There was a marriage and a divorce. She went from being debt-free to owing places she'd never stepped into. Change seemed to be her middle name these days.

"Change is inevitable." She turned to look at the plastic floral monstrosity that took up the entire six-foot-wide table in the entry. "I think we'll get rid of that."

Liz hopped up and down. "Oh good. I saw a mouse crawl out of it the other day."

A shiver ran down Danielle's spine. Rodents weren't her thing. "Did you call Todd?"

She blushed, "Yes, and he told me to stop pretending there were mice, and to ask him out if that's what I wanted."

"Oh. Wow." She mindlessly straightened the brochures on the counter. "Is that what you want?"

Her expression turned soft. "He is dreamy."

She couldn't argue. Todd was a handsome man. He did a good job with the resources he had and was a magician with a toolbox and duct tape.

"Then you should ask him out."

"I already did. We're having a drink after work. I'm taking him to Powders."

"Have fun, and don't worry. Everything here will get better."

"How do you know?"

"I have a feeling." What she felt resembled acid reflux, but employee morale was important.

She rushed to the elevator. Answering her usual daily mountain of emails made the top of her to-do list, right after hitting the lounge for a cup of dark roast happiness. Her morning cup had never hit her lips, and the coffee at the meeting was barely drinkable. It needed at least six tablespoons of sugar to cut the bitterness. When Julian laid only a handful of packets on the table, she knew she'd have to suffer through it. Pouring it and not drinking it would have been rude.

The elevator lurched to her floor. A cloud of dust floated around her as she exited and walked toward her desk.

Email first, and then coffee.

Ding, ding, ding, ding rang out as she powered up her computer. Her inbox lit up with messages. Several were from other department heads.

It wasn't a surprise. Somehow, she was the go-to for all concerns and complaints. Avis made herself unavailable, and somehow Danielle had ended up her surrogate. She ran the reports, attended the meetings, and took care of employee complaints.

"No wonder she left. If asked to bring a list of accomplishments, Avis would have one entry. She hired me. I did her damn job."

The first email was from Willetta, who asked how she could improve her chances of keeping her job.

Everyone loves you. You'll be fine.

Danielle

The next email came from Paul, in Security, asking for suggestions to impress the new owners.

She had a lot of suggestions that started with washing his uniform. Since housekeeping was in charge of employee uniforms, he had no excuse for looking slovenly. Hiding somewhere during the day was a problem too. He was never in his cubicle or the surveillance room. She had a feeling he hung out where they kept the overstock and slept on the new mattresses.

Get a fresh uniform and make yourself seen.

Danielle

She saw a message from Chris but ignored it. She moved through her emails.

A cloud of dust whooshed through her space, and the thunder of hammers and the squeal of saws was all she heard.

"Holy hell. What is going on here?"

She'd cleared her emails but one, and reluctantly opened the message from her ex. All it said was, *You'll be working for me soon.*

"Not likely." She saw the way they watched everyone in the room. While Chris was a chameleon, she had to hope Allie and Julian saw past his façade. Honestly, if they looked past his movie-star smile, he'd be lucky to keep his job.

She prayed that he wouldn't lose it. His car was the only thing he paid for from their marital debt, and that was because she told him if she made the payment the car was hers. But if he was out of a job, he couldn't pay for it, and as his co-signer, she'd be stuck with the bill.

She lowered her head into her hands. She was thirty-five and in debt up to her ears because she believed in love. When she said I do, it meant forever. When Chris said those words, it meant until he found something shinier.

A big boom shook the walls of the offices. She pushed back and rose from her chair. No way would she get the orders put in if she couldn't think. She marched down the hall toward the commotion. There was no longer a door to Avis's office but a large gaping hole in the wall.

A man stood with his back to her, a yellow hard hat on. He directed the workers like a drill sergeant. She recognized the voice.

A single tap on his shoulder had him spinning around to face her. "This is a construction zone; you'll need a hat to be in here." He took the one from his head and placed it on hers.

She stepped back. "This is a work zone." She waved her hands around. "Why couldn't this have happened earlier?"

"Scheduling conflict." He shrugged as if her complaint had no merit. "Why couldn't you do your office work earlier?"

She handed the safety hat back to him. "Scheduling conflict." She said and pivoted on her heels to trudge toward the employee lounge. When she got there, nothing remained but wires and pipes.

"Where is the coffee?!" she screamed, if only to hear herself over the noise. Her day teetered on the edge of bad, ready to plummet toward worse.

James walked up beside her. "I hear the restaurant downstairs serves a decent cup." He picked up a roll of plastic sheeting and walked toward the area where her cubicle stood.

Furious, she stomped past him to her desk. "I don't have time for field trips. I've got reports to run, orders to place, and a nervous breakdown to fit in between customer complaints and employee reviews."

She pulled out her chair and flopped onto the tattered cushion. The old springs creaked as she rocked back and forth. It was a subtle way to release pent up frustration. The movement was soothing despite the sound, which she hardly heard over the construction and stapling of plastic sheeting behind her.

She twisted to watch him staple her inside. "That's not helping," she called out.

He peeked around the edge. "You'll love me later when there's minimal dust in your workspace."

"Don't get your hopes up. I'm a hard sell on love." All at once, the room went silent. She was certain the only thing she heard was the dust settling and the rustling of her plastic prison walls. "Thank God." She returned to her computer. When she moved her mouse, there was nothing. Not a flicker of light. Not a word. Not a sound. It was heaven and hell combined.

"Tripped a breaker," someone yelled from down the hallway.

She threw up her hands. "You've got to be kidding me." Jumping from her seat, she went to see what could be done to get the power turned back on, but she hit a wall of plastic. James had stapled her inside.

"Hello," she called out. No one answered. She considered taking scissors and cutting her way free, but was it wise to piss off the guy in charge of building her office?

No coffee and no escape. The only thing left was to review the printed profit-and-loss statements from the various departments that Avis had her analyzing before she left.

No one stood out as a thief. Much of what she saw were simple oversights. Ordering based on last year's numbers when this year's occupancy rate was down by twenty-five percent. Given that Luxe closed off the tower for the summer to remodel, it only reduced their income potential further. She understood the need to have the building vacant, especially now that she'd heard the noise and was living without electricity.

Back at her desk, she moved her pen down the reports. Reports she had no business seeing since they belonged to other departments.

Maybe it was good that Avis left because Danielle could get back to doing her job and only her job. For months she'd been taking on more while Avis did less. That made her an easy choice for general manager because she already did the work. But her late arrival and her appearance erased any grand illusion of a promotion. Besides, she didn't want a job that would put her in a no-win situation with her ex-husband. She could see it now; Chris would question every decision she made then complain to the higher-ups. If she gave him a poor rating, he'd say it was her bitterness, not his performance.

She pulled out his half-finished quarterly report. Outdoor recreation was the most expensive department in the resort, which never made sense. How many fishing rods, flies, snowshoes, and paddle boards did he need? Maybe she was too hard on him. Guests were tough on everything from bedding to baths. No one treated a hotel like *their* home. The average person wouldn't drink wine in bed or drag their bag across the carpet, pulling at the fibers.

She pinched the bridge of her nose. When this became all-inclusive, it would be worse. For many, all-inclusive meant anything goes.

The lights above her flickered, and the hum of the central air conditioning filled the air. This was perfect if everything else remained silent. She pulled up the reports on her computer and scanned the entries. It wasn't her job to analyze, just get the numbers, and they were dismal.

Out of habit, she reached for her cup, which wasn't there.

"I'd kill for a cup of coffee."

"You don't have to," James said from behind the plastic.

She turned to face his shadowy figure and watched him cut a

slice in the sheet from ceiling to floor. "Sorry I locked you in. The guys tripped the breaker, and I had to see Todd in Engineering." He pushed through and walked forward, carrying two cups of steaming coffee. "While I was there, I got this." He passed her the mug.

She didn't know if she was grateful or annoyed. He was the reason she didn't have coffee in the first place.

"Thanks." She said, resigned to be appreciative.

"You're welcome." He looked over her shoulder. "What are you doing now?"

"Pulling together the profit-and-loss reports."

He lifted his brows and leaned in so close she could smell the fabric softener in his shirt.

"Is that your job? I thought you'd only be responsible for your department." He stared at her glowing computer monitor. "By the looks of it, you're doing everyone's reports."

She turned around and flicked off the power to her screen. "This isn't your job either. Shouldn't you be giving me permanent hearing loss from your nonstop drilling and hammering? I'm assuming the breaker's fixed since my equipment is working."

He straightened and leaned against the partition dividing her cubicle from Paul's. "Everyone is taking a coffee break. Why are you doing all the reports?"

A heavy sigh emptied her. "Avis was a delegator."

He shook his head. "Basically, you did her job."

"Of course not. I helped run the reports and order supplies."

"Right." He nodded to the coffee in her hand. "You gonna drink that?"

"Yes." Tentatively, she brought the cup to her lips. Expecting the bitterness to bite her tongue, the sweetness coating her taste buds was a surprise. "It's good." She smiled.

"I got it right?"

She laughed. "It could be sweeter."

He kicked off the divider. "So could you." He winked and walked away.

Chapter 6

JAMES

James looked at his watch. Time for coffee. He rushed out of the resort to go to the barista across the street. The coffee in the restaurant was decent, but it didn't have the kick he needed. He was sure Danielle would appreciate a nice strong brew too since they tore apart the lounge several days before. Running crews 24/7 made everything happen quickly.

He ordered two double shot Americanos. While he waited, he filled his pockets with sugar packets.

It had been two days since he'd seen her. She spent a great deal of time mentoring her employees and mingling with the guests. The only time she was in the office was at the start and the end of the day.

On the other hand, he'd seen a lot of the other department heads, who seemed to camp at their desks eating and internet shopping. Only Danielle, Willetta, and Flynn appeared to work.

"Order for James."

He walked to the counter to pick up the cups. A hand reached out to take one.

"How sweet." Allie's hand skimmed the coffee cup before he snatched it away.

"Sorry, this one's not for you."

Her precision plucked brow lifted. "Interesting." She pointed to the line. "Wait for me." She ordered her standard cup of nothing—a fat-free, sugar-free, caffeine-free latte.

Standing by him, she eyed the coffees but said nothing. "I got the weekly reports for the departments. It's grim."

He kicked back against the counter. "Did you know Danielle put those reports together?"

Allie smiled. "Is that why they're so good? I couldn't imagine Paul delivering anything so comprehensive. She even calculates week-to-week, month-to-month, and year-to-year changes."

"Turns out she's been running things for Avis for a long time."

"When did you find that out?" She reached for a napkin and a stir stick.

"The day I accidentally plastic-wrapped her into the room with the cubicles." Thankfully, the focus of her anger was the lack of coffee and not being trapped inside.

"How did that go over?"

"She was remarkably nice considering we'd accidentally cut the power too."

"Way to make friends."

"Order for Allie," the barista called out.

She grabbed her coffee, and they walked out of the shop into the sun. Spring in the Rockies was always perfect. High on the peaks, the snow glistened white while at slightly lower elevations, flowers popped through the soil and the Aspens began to bud. James loved the spring. It was a time for fresh starts. A time for hopes to come to fruition. Luxe would be a huge success ... he hoped.

"Have you heard from Greed lately?" Allie asked.

Leave it to his sister to place a cloud over him. "Hell no. She took her settlement and left for warmer weather. I hear she's in Phoenix."

Allie laughed. "She'll need the settlement for cosmetic surgery. That sun and dry climate will ruin her skin. I see fillers and Botox coming her way."

James didn't want to talk about his ex-wife. "I don't care if her face falls off." She had stopped being beautiful the day she left him. "I'm just glad she moved far away." Grace, who his family renamed Greed after the divorce, milked him for over a million. It was a small price to pay to get his life back.

With her gone, he could spend time in Aspen again. Years ago, he owned a house and called Aspen home. Once he and Grace's relationship fell apart, he stayed away as much as possible to avoid her. Funny how absence caused his marital problems and solved them at the same time.

"What about you?" He and Allie were both staying together at their father's winter vacation home but rarely found the time to talk about silly things like relationships. "Anyone new in your life?"

She nearly tripped when her heel caught in a crack in the sidewalk. "Nope. After the last disaster, I'm happy to stay single."

"Me too."

She laughed. "We're both such good liars, I'd almost believe us. Who would think having money would be such an issue?"

They entered the massive glass doors of Luxe. He was pleased to see they were smudge-free and sparkled like a diamond.

"Good call on the plastic floral monstrosity." James walked to the round walnut table and smelled the fresh flowers. The arrangement was large, but it didn't block the view to the registration desk, the new chandelier, or the plush couches in the common area. "What's this pink and white one that smells so good?"

"It's a stargazer lily. They last a long time too."

Allie's heels clicked on the marble floor as they headed toward the elevator. Funny how he could recognize the distinctive staccato of her walk.

The car appeared, and they entered. There wasn't any traffic to the now vacant tower, and an eerie silence blanketed them.

As the door closed, a voice called for them to wait.

With hands full, James stuck his boot between the doors to open them back up.

Danielle rushed in. "Sorry for the delay." She was breathless.

He handed her the cup of coffee, "This is for you."

Her eyes grew wide. "Umm ... thank you. That was kind."

Allie's eyes nearly popped from their sockets.

He pressed the buttons for the twelfth and thirteenth floor.

"Interesting," Allie said as she exited on twelve.

Danielle stepped forward and asked. "Is there something I can do for you? Did you want to get into any of the rooms?"

Allie held up her key. "Nope. I've got it under control. Until we finish the offices, I'll hole up here."

Danielle stepped back inside, and the doors closed. "I didn't know she was staying in the hotel."

James rested against the wall. "Is that a problem? It makes sense for her to be close to work."

At the next stop, they exited, and he followed her to her desk.

At the first sip of her coffee, she frowned, and he laughed. After balancing his coffee on the edge of the cubicle divider, he dug into his pocket for the sugar packets. He laid no less than twenty on her desk.

Her giggle filled the quiet room. "You'd make a good drug mule."

"I don't think they shove that stuff in their pockets."

Her cheeks blushed pink. "You're right. I'd stick to what you do."

"Driving you crazy with dust and noise?"

She shrugged. "Better than shoving stuff up your ..." She shook her head. "Not a good vision."

He turned around and looked at his ass. "Never had complaints before."

"Forget it." She waved her hand toward the slit in the plastic. "Get to work so I can too." She emptied the sugar into her coffee, and the next sip brought a smile to her face. "Americano? How did you know?"

He was pleased he'd gotten it right. His track record with women wasn't all that good.

"I didn't. It's what I like, only I prefer a little sugar in my coffee, not a little coffee in my sugar."

"I've got a sweet tooth."

"You've got an addiction." He was almost to the plastic when she called him back.

"When will you complete the lounge?"

"I thought you liked my gift."

She stood and looked at him. "I do, but you're right, I have an addiction, and I need several of these a day. Thanks for the first one."

"Bet you had two at home before you came to work."

She held up three fingers. "You're close. With all the changes happening, I needed more."

He knew his brows were furled because of the strain between them. "Is the change all that bad?"

She took a few seconds to answer. "Not sure yet. It's unsettling to not know where I stand. Eventually, they'll choose a new general manager, and that will bring more disruption."

He walked back and laid his hand on her shoulder. "Don't worry. Sometimes change is exactly what we need." Her blue, button-down felt silky under his fingertips. Would her skin be as soft? He glanced at her lips, so full and pink. Would they?

"We'll see," she said.

He stepped back. There was something about her he liked. Was it her drive? The way she appeared tough and vulnerable at the same time? The way she refused to make excuses for herself? Maybe it was the light floral scent of her perfume.

"I think you'll be okay. You appear to be proficient at your job and everyone else's."

She leaned forward and looked at him like he was a science project—a germ in a Petri dish. "A compliment from you? The man who told me I should know about the secret love nest tucked behind the general manager's office?"

"I was wrong."

She picked up a pen and notepad. "Let me jot this down. James was wrong." She said the words as she wrote them. "Can I get you to initial this so people know it's real?"

"Now you're a comedian?"

She tossed the pen and pad on her desk. "Jack of all trades. Master of none." She reached for her coffee. "You never answered my question. When will you finish the lounge?"

"End of next week. We're making it a fully functional kitchen with working appliances and everything. It will have a microwave from this century."

"What about the apartment?"

"Gone except for a small studio in case the new general manager needs to stay the night."

She walked toward the plastic and ducked between the opening.

"That's a shame. I loved that floor."

"I'll try to repurpose it just for you." He turned left, and she turned right. "By the way," he called over his shoulder. "I hear there will be a potluck for the lounge opening. The new owners are supplying lunch, and the department heads will bring dessert."

"How do you know that?"

He shouldn't know anything, but he did. "Allie told me today when I saw her at the coffee shop. You know how to cook, right?"

"Oh, yeah. I'm a master cake maker." Her head movement shook from left to right while her words claimed yes. He wondered if she realized it.

"Great, can't wait to taste what you're making."

Chapter 7

DANIELLE

The email came in at lunch when Danielle was covering the registration desk for an employee with an emergency. She'd read it three times.

Let's celebrate. Lunch is on us. Dessert is on you. Cakes, cookies, or pies. Whatever you like. Time to impress us with your culinary skills.

Allie and Julian

Alistair, the other partner, wasn't mentioned. No doubt still overseeing another project. She pulled up all their bios on the company website. They were missing pictures. Inside the blocks it said, *Coming Soon*. What would an Alistair look like? The name conjured either a yuppie in a suit and no socks or a dork with a comb-over hiding his shiny bald spot.

There was no time to think about him and search further when she needed to figure out where to buy an impressive dessert.

How was she supposed impress anyone with her culinary skills when she couldn't make toast? When she was a kid and burned the bread, her mother used to tell her to scrape it until it became the color she liked.

She did her usual routine when anxiety struck; she called Trish.

"Where can I get a cake that will impress?"

"Impress who?"

"Does it matter?" She straightened the guest brochures.

"Yes. Especially if Connie's Confections, your standard go-to isn't suitable."

"I need to make something for my bosses. They're asking us to impress them with our culinary skills."

"You can't claim skill if you buy a cake. Make it."

She leaned against the counter. "You know I can't cook."

Trish cleared her throat. "Perfect time to use those books. You know the ones that are probably still in the back of your SUV."

"I brought one in." The heart book sat on her counter still untouched, but it was inside her home.

"Shocking."

"Whatever. Can you get a kitchen pass to come over? I'll give it a go but if it's awful, I'll need a backup."

"Do you need the cake by tomorrow?"

"No, but I need to practice so I don't kill anyone."

Trish laughed. "This is something I have to see. I'll even opt-out of sexy time with Rob to watch this train wreck. Let me make sure your policy is up to date."

"Haha." Trish owned the insurance company Danielle used. "If I burn down the house, I want a high estimate for repairs."

"You'll get what's fair."

"Speaking of fair, I saved you from a claim on my car. This time someone hit me instead of the other way around."

"Someone hit you? Are you okay?"

"Yes, I'm fine. It's a long story, but all you need to know is since he hit me, he was at fault."

"And your car?"

"A little ding in the bumper."

"Whew, you can't afford a rate hike."

"Tell me about it."

"What time do you want me to come over?"

"I need supplies. What does it take to bake a cake?"

Trish laughed. "I have no idea. I buy my cakes at Connie's. Text me when you're home." She hung up before Danielle could comment.

It was well after six when she pulled into the local grocery store. She preferred it to the big chains. Going to the small store was like visiting friends. Everyone knew each other.

"Evening, Danielle," Betty Davenport said as she entered. "You coming for frozen pizza or the egg salad sandwich tonight?"

Had she become that predictable? What had she eaten the night before? *Egg salad.* She let out a groan.

"I need whatever it takes to bake a cake."

Betty's forehead wrinkled with the lift of her brow. "You bakin'?"

"That's the plan." She pulled a grocery cart from the stack lined up by the door and moved forward.

Betty left her spot at the register and walked to where Danielle stood.

"What kind of cake?"

Could a head explode—literally explode? Danielle's felt like hers might pop any minute. She didn't make cakes. She ate them. If the dimple on her right butt cheek was an indicator, she ate too many. Or ... maybe that was from the mound of sugar she put in her coffee.

"No idea. Aren't they all about the same?"

"No. There's apple spice and orange and cinnamon cakes. There are speckled birthday cakes like the ice cream you eat by the gallon. There's white cake and yellow and chocolate cake. What about red velvet?"

She didn't know what was in the cookbook.

"My head hurts. Can you help me get the basics or the stuff required to make several varieties?"

"What about a boxed cake? All you need is the mix and a can of frosting, plus water, oil, and eggs."

It would be an easy out, but wouldn't that be the same as buying one? Danielle never quit anything she started, which was why her divorce was so painful.

"I'm making it. Set me up with everything I might need."

Thirty minutes later, she walked out of the store with two bags of baking supplies and a frozen pizza.

She sent a text to Trish and told her it was time. An immediate reply said to get started without her because they moved up sexy time, and she'd be over within the hour.

An hour? Chris never lasted an hour.

"Some girls have all the luck."

She carried in the supplies and stared at them sitting on her counter. Half of the ingredients were foreign. What the hell was baking chocolate?

She unwrapped the corner of the bar and took a bite. Immediately, she spit it into a nearby napkin.

"Gross."

Next, she opened the bag of chocolate chips. While she ate a handful, she peeked inside the cookbook.

There was a preface. A hand-written note on the inside front cover. This wasn't a store-bought book, but one passed down from generation to generation. If the smudges and stains spoke to its age, it was ancient and well used.

Dear Baker,

Everything I learned about love, I learned from baking.

Everything you need to know about love, you'll learn here.

Because you're reading this, it means you've accepted the challenge of choosing one recipe, perfecting it, and passing on the book.

As with everything in life, baking takes effort. Like love, it can't be rushed.

Have you ever wondered why baked goods require certain ingredients?

We add sugar to bring out our inner sweetness.

Salt gives life its flavor.

Flour is a binder like honesty and faithfulness.

Butter is the guilty pleasure in the mix.

Baking soda lifts like a bright smile on a dull day.

Without these, a cake is not a cake, and a pie not a pie. Without love, a life isn't worth living.

Baking, like love, should be done with passion.

I challenge you to pick one recipe and only one because love shouldn't be hoarded but shared.

Choose the right recipe, and if you can't decide, open the book to a page and let the recipe choose you.

Share the dessert but not the book. There will be time for that later.

Remember, a perfect cake, or pie, or cookie is like perfect love. It's takes practice, patience, give and take, resourcefulness, perseverance, and often teamwork.

With love,

Adelaide Phelps

"I failed at love. Let's hope I have more success with baking a cake." She turned the page to find a handwritten index listing dozens of recipes with names like:

Cherish Me Cheesecake

Crave Me Cupcakes

Indulge Your Desire Date Bars

Friendly Fruitcake

Comfort Me Carrot Cake

Slow Burn Blondie

Romantic Flame Flan

Passion Pillow Cookies

Finally, there was one that caught her eye—Forever Fudge Cake. She popped a few more chocolate chips into her mouth. She skipped the story above the recipe and went straight to gathering the ingredients. The name was perfect because she knew she would regret this endeavor forever.

When she got to the Baker's chocolate, she shook her head. Nothing containing that could be good, so she substituted the vile stuff with the dark chocolate chips.

"Hello," Trish called from the door.

Danielle yelled back. "In the kitchen."

Her friend didn't have to knock because she had a key, and there wouldn't be any kitchen acrobatics happening in Danielle's house. Her counter was strictly for bills and take and bake pizza.

Trish strolled into the kitchen, all sex blushed and smiling, while Danielle poured the cake into pans.

Thankfully, Peggy added them to her supplies. And if Trish hadn't bought her measuring spoons and cups at the flea market, she would have had to guess. Guessing was never a strength for her.

"Where's the apron I got you?"

Danielle pointed to the hook on the wall. "Didn't want to get my hopes up that maybe spooning would lead to forking or maybe porking."

"Just wear it and leave the pork out, no swine for me. There's plenty of fun with forking."

Trish dipped her finger into the batter and sucked it off. She immediately grabbed a napkin, and after a few gagging noises, she wiped off her tongue.

"Stop goofing around. I followed the recipe. It should be amazing."

"Amazing if you like the taste of monkey butt." Trish went to the drawer where the corkscrew was and opened the bottle of wine she brought. She poured two glasses, sipped from one, and gargled. "That's vile."

"When have you ever had monkey butt?"

Trish plopped onto the stool at the counter. "Never, but I'm sure that's what it would taste like. How's work?"

Danielle set the timer and picked up her glass, moving to the living room. Her place was an open cottage concept. It was small but quaint. She'd worked hard to get a homey feel with soft colors and floral chintz pillows. She might not cook, but she had great taste in furnishings.

"It's hell, and not only because I have to make a cake."

Trish flopped on the couch next to her. "Tell me."

She started with the first meeting, her being late, and the coffee spill debacle.

"Way to make a good first impression. Tell me more."

"One of the owner's name is Allie. She's cool. I like her, but she's staying in the hotel. I didn't even know it. Shouldn't I know those things?"

"If she's in the tower, then it's no biggie. Didn't you say they were starting at the top and working their way down? She's not hurting your ability to rent the rooms."

Trish had a point, but not knowing made her feel out of the loop. She hated it when people weren't upfront and honest. Transparency was important.

"Then there's the guy who's in charge of construction. Honestly, he knows more than I do, and that drives me nuts. It's like Allie tells him everything and me nothing. He walks around the place like he owns it."

"Maybe they've worked together for a long time. Him knowing stuff isn't a crime. What else?"

"A couple of days ago, he brought me a coffee from downstairs. Today, he showed up with a coffee from Pikes Perk and about twenty packets of sugar."

"Yeah. He's a real jerk." Trish snorted. "You know, not every guy is like Chris. Some are good. Take Rob for instance."

Danielle sighed and leaned against the soft cushions. "We can't all marry the bagel king."

Trish smiled. "I know. I got lucky. He's got a nice bagel, and his lox aren't bad either."

"Stop bragging about his bagel."

"Stop being cynical. You're young and beautiful."

Danielle knuckled her tired eyes. "I'll die alone."

"No way. What kind of cat do you want?"

"I'm allergic to cats. I'll be the crazy cake lady instead." She leaned forward to grab her wine and emptied the contents in one swallow. She lifted her nose. Chocolate and sugar scented the air. "Monkey butt my ass. That smells amazing." The timer went off, and they both raced to the kitchen.

Danielle donned mitts and pulled the pans from the oven. As soon as she saw the cakes, her heart sank. The cracked tops made them look like they'd baked in the desert for a week.

"Maybe it tastes better than it looks," she said.

"I'm telling you," Trish said. "the batter tasted like monkey back hole."

Danielle cut a piece and pulled it from the pan. It was rock hard, and heavy. When she dropped it on a nearby paper plate, the slice broke in two.

"You promised to be my taste tester."

Trish looked at the plate. "That was before. Now, I'm afraid. I'd rather eat the plate." She picked up the smallest piece and put it into her mouth.

Danielle leaned forward, waiting for the verdict. "What do you think?"

Trish swallowed hard like it was a golf ball instead of a bite of dessert.

"I've had fluffier, more flavorful matzo. Eh." Trish made a sound like she was hacking up a hairball. "You have some time to perfect it." She picked up the wine and drank straight from the bottle. "Next week, let's go back to the flea market and get you that cross-stitch kit."

She pointed to the ingredients that covered her counter. "I'm baking cakes for my hobby. Why would I get a cross-stitch kit?"

Trish moved back. "Cross-stitch won't kill me."

Chapter 8

JAMES

Today was the third day he'd arrived with two cups of coffee and a pocket filled with sugar packets. Danielle was already at her desk, organizing her day. She had a planner she carried with her all the time. In a tidy straight line, she wrote out everything she had to accomplish for the day. Items she deemed a priority got a star.

He snuck up on her and leaned over her chair, casting a shadow across the pages.

"What are you doing here?"

He moved to her side and leaned against the cubicle divider.

"How did you know it was me?"

"I could smell you." She turned her head and smiled.

He wasn't sure if that was a put-down or a compliment. "Should I be offended?"

"Do you think you smell bad?"

He offered her a cup and pulled the sugar packets from his pockets.

"Do you?"

She rolled back and took him in. He loved the way she always stared at him. He felt like a pastry in the display case. It was as if she craved what she saw but didn't dare indulge.

"You smell better than the guys working for you. Do they shower?"

"Can't say. Their personal hygiene has never been my focus."

"What is your focus?" She closed her planner and emptied a dozen sugars into her coffee. After her first drink, she smiled and sighed. "So good. Thank you."

He pointed to her face. "That, right there, is my first goal of every day. Your smile makes the wait in line at Pikes Perk worth it."

"I don't know why you do it, but I won't complain."

"I do it because losing the lounge temporarily made your life worse." He looked over his shoulder as if he could see the old lounge through the plastic sheeting. "Although, how you got a decent cup out of that old pot was a mystery."

"Beggars can't be choosers."

He kicked off the wall. "Then stop being a beggar and be a chooser."

With her coffee in her hand, she lifted from her chair. "I need to make my rounds."

"Which is another reason I'm here. I want to show you what's finished. Do you have time?"

She stalled for a moment, and he thought she might say no. Instead, she shrugged on her blazer, and with her coffee and planner in hand, she moved to the split in the plastic.

Once in the corridor, he placed his palm at the small of her back and guided her toward the new offices.

"Oh, wow. You really changed the place around." She moved along the new hallway that had one large office on the right and smaller offices on the left.

"This one will be the general manager's." He walked into the nearly finished room. All it needed was a door and a paint job.

She tapped her heel against the marble floor. "You saved it." She lowered to her haunches and ran her fingers across the shiny surface.

"I knew you loved it, so I saved enough to do this office and the studio."

"I'm glad, the stone was too beautiful to toss away." She moved around the spacious room.

It wasn't the cavernous hole it had been when he started the project, but it was an ample size for the position.

"You want to see the studio?"

"Sure." She followed him through the door at the rear of the office. "Wow."

He tried to look at it through her eyes. The posh two-bedroom apartment that was once here was gone, but this was high-end and fully equipped.

"It's small but efficient. I think whoever gets this space will be happy here."

A floor to ceiling divider hid the full-sized bed on one half of the room. A living room was set up with a big-screen TV that took up the bulk of the rest of the space. There was even a wall that acted as a compact kitchen. It replicated the lounge, but the studio had a barista-worthy coffee machine. He was considering one for the lounge but wasn't sure the department heads could operate it.

"Does it come with a person to make the coffee?"

"No." He pulled out a drawer and took out a packet of papers. "It comes with a manual."

"Good enough."

They left the manager's space and walked into the offices across the hall.

"These are for the owners."

"They're smaller than the managers. Won't that be a problem?"

"I don't see why. They don't need much space."

She went from room to room. "Will all three of them work here?"

"Yes."

"Where will the department heads work? Are you going to leave the cubicles as they are?"

"Hell no. That whole workspace is atrocious. I'm surprised

anyone gets anything done there. That area will be a conference room. The only time department heads will be on this floor is to have lunch and for meetings."

She came to a halt. "Oh ... where will we do our reports?"

"Everyone can use the computers in the conference room. Each department head will have a space in their work zone. For example, the perfect space for your job would be around the registration desk. You spend most of your days there or on the floors anyway, so it won't be a great loss. As for the others ... maybe they'll work more."

She laughed. "You've noticed."

"I don't miss much."

"Speaking of work. I need to go. Thanks for the tour." She headed toward the hallway.

"Wait up. What about lunch? Can I take you to lunch?"

He watched as her cheeks turned pink.

"I work through lunch."

"Okay then. What about a drink after work?"

She smiled. "I'm flattered, but dating people I work with isn't a good idea."

He agreed with that policy, but they didn't work together. He was in charge of construction.

"It's a drink, not a date. Just two people relaxing after a long day." *Say yes. Say yes. Say yes.*

Her expression remained resolute for about ten seconds, and then a smile lifted the corners of her lips. "Okay. One drink and I'm buying since you've bought the coffee all week."

His heart swelled with joy. "Deal. How about Halfpipe? It's a few doors down and has great craft beer and mean martinis."

"What about wine?"

He pushed the elevator button for her. "I'm sure they've got that too. Meet you there at five?"

She glanced at her planner. "Make it six, and it's a date." She laughed. "Not a real date." She looked to the ceiling. "You know what I mean."

He smiled. "Yeah. It's a date."

He turned around and nearly skipped back to work. Danielle didn't consider it a date, but something inside him said it was.

HE WATCHED THE DOOR, waiting for her. Halfpipe wasn't packed, but it was hopping.

When she entered, all the tension in his body left. He wasn't sure if it was because he'd been protecting her seat like it was a crown jewel or because she actually showed up. He hadn't been certain she would.

"Glad you came."

"I said I would. I always do what I say."

"Good to know there are still honest people out there."

The bartender came over. "What's your poison?"

"Do you have a decent cabernet?"

He laid down a napkin. "I've got a cabernet. Not sure if it's decent, but it's red."

"I'll take it."

James sipped his locally brewed beer and watched her. Dark brown strands once tucked into the bun at the base of her neck now framed her face. Danielle was beautiful in an understated way. He was certain when she scrubbed off her makeup, she'd still be stunning.

"While you look lovely after working a ten-hour day, I'll bet you're tired," he said.

"When did you become an expert on me?" She rubbed the dark circles below her eyes.

"I told you earlier, I notice a lot."

"No ... you said you don't miss much."

"Same difference."

The bartender set her wine down and walked away.

James picked up his beer. "Here's to friends who aren't on a date." He waited for her to pick up her glass and tap his.

"Here's to something." She tipped it back and took a long swallow.

"You want to talk about it?"

She let out a breath that vibrated her partially closed lips. "I don't know where to start."

"How about with your biggest worry?"

"Every time I turn around, I'm worried about losing my job." She pulled the napkin from under her wine glass and shredded it into confetti.

He leaned in until the scent of her perfume was all he could smell. "Why would you think that?"

"You want a list? How about I give you the bullet points?" She started ticking them off on her fingers. "New owners. New general manager. Lots of changes. Hell, they didn't even tell me they were already working from the hotel."

"Well, they have to work from somewhere while the offices are being completed."

"True, but they claim to be like family with their first name basis bullshit and potluck celebrations. Wouldn't family let you know what's going on?"

"Maybe nothing is going on that needs sharing."

She took another deep drink of her wine, nearly emptying the glass. "You know how dogs eat their young if they're not perfect?"

He narrowed his eyes. "Where are you going with this?"

"I feel like I'm about to be gobbled up."

Without thought, he put his palm on her knee. For a moment, when she glanced down, he thought she'd brush him away, but she didn't. Instead, she covered his hand with hers and left it there.

"Personally, I don't believe you have anything to worry about. You and Flynn and Willetta and Chris are about the only people who do their jobs."

"You think Chris does his job? You're not nearly as observant as you think."

"I haven't seen him in action, but he's seems put together and a tad bit cocky. You on the other hand seem to have it under control."

"I appreciate you saying that, but what you see doesn't matter. What if they're not looking? What if they're the type to not notice? What if I am a fatality of the takeover?"

"What if you're the best thing they've seen in a long time?"

She let her head fall forward. "Yeah, what if ..."

He pulled his hand from below hers and raised her chin. "You're amazing." He stared into her eyes. Eyes that showed her boiling pot of emotions.

She gave him a weak smile. "I'm a work in progress."

"You're perfect the way you are." He sipped his beer. "Hey, I'm finishing the lounge in a few days. Are you excited?"

"Does that mean you'll stop bringing me coffee?"

"Would you like me to bring you coffee?" Watching her smile each time he handed her a cup was the highlight of his day. He didn't have to do it. She didn't expect it, but the unexpected made life exciting.

"I wouldn't send you away."

"Good to know." He finished his beer. "Do you want another drink?"

She shook her head. "I better not. That potluck is coming, and I need to prepare."

"What are you making?"

"A cake."

"How hard could that be?"

She pulled a twenty from her wallet and set it on the counter.

"Depends on the goal. Should it be edible? Or, should I shoot for something that won't kill anyone?"

He laughed. "You're kidding, right?"

She stood. "Yes. I make a mean cake. The trick to perfection is in the planning."

"Let me walk you back." He slid from the stool.

"No need. I found my way here, and I'll find my way back."

"Call me old fashioned, but I insist."

They walked side-by-side back to Luxe. He made sure to walk a little too closely, so their hands grazed with each stride. That simple touch sent a jolt of electricity to his once numb heart. Warmth spread through his chest. It felt good—damn good.

He made sure she got into her car safely and watched her drive away. When he glanced at his watch, he groaned. It was only seven o'clock. There were a dozen hours before he'd see her again.

Women were all kinds of trouble. Would Danielle be the good kind?

Chapter 9

DANIELLE

She set all the ingredients out and took inventory to make sure she had everything she needed.

To anyone on the outside, it would appear as if she was readying herself for something monumental. Something like open-heart surgery.

She tied on the apron and stared at the oil and sugar and salt, hoping to bake them into submission.

The minute she opened the flour, her phone rang, and the screen lit up with Trish's smiling face.

"Can't talk. I'm getting ready to dive into baking again."

"That's my girl. Fail once, try again. Fail twice; maybe you should buy the cake."

"Quit it. I'm determined to master this baking thing."

"I'll be right over."

Before Danielle could say no, Trish had hung up.

To build her courage, she pulled a bottle of wine from the rack and poured herself a glass. She needed to have one down to deal with Trish and the pressure of baking the perfect cake.

Ten minutes later, her friend rushed into the kitchen.

"Am I too late to see the disaster?"

Danielle flicked a teaspoon of flour at Trish, and it dusted her dark hair.

"Why did you do that?"

"Why did you come over? This is hard enough without you making fun of me."

"I'm not making fun of you. I'm finding the humor in your mess."

"Not helping."

Trish grabbed a glass and poured herself some wine. "Like I said before, no one can ignore a train wreck. Besides, I have an investment in your hobby." She pointed to the apron. "I bought the uniform and some equipment."

"Fine. Sit down. If you're here, you need to be a taster."

Trish reached into her bag and pulled out a jumbo-sized bottle of antacids. "I came prepared."

With the recipe book folded open to show only the cake she was working on, Danielle followed the directions to a T.

"Does it say rounded cupfuls? What about rounded teaspoonfuls?" Trish piped in.

"No, but if the ratio is the same, what does it matter?"

"Size matters, Danielle. Everyone knows that. It's the universal truth about everything, including diamonds, cups of flour, and penises."

"I'm only dealing with flour, so let me do my thing while you ponder the others." She mixed the dry and the wet ingredients together.

"How's the construction hottie?"

"Who said he was hot?"

Trish talked with her hands, which sliced through the air like sharp daggers. "You've mentioned him before, so there must be something good about him."

Danielle poured the batter into the pans. "I haven't found him naked and doing someone on the counter."

"That was only once. Get over it." Trish reached into the bag of chocolate chips and took several. "Tell me more about him. James, right?"

"He still brings me coffee every morning."

Trish sat up taller. "That's commitment. Tell me more?"

Danielle slid the pans into the preheated oven and set the timer. "He showed me the new offices."

"Your new office?"

"No, the new general manager and the owners." Remembering the marble floor, she smiled. "He repurposed the old flooring because I loved it."

Trish nearly spit out her just sipped wine. "That old confetti colored carpet? That stuff is hideous."

Danielle walked around the island and perched herself on the end stool. "No, it's a beautiful white marble with veins of gold."

"I think he likes you."

Did she dare say they had a date that wasn't actually a date? It sure felt like one. Especially when he cupped her knee with his palm. The man was a live wire, and his touch made her hair stand up—in a good way.

"I think you're right, but it doesn't matter because I'll never date someone I work with again."

"You don't work with him."

"That's what he said." Danielle left her chair and pulled out a box of cold pizza from the fridge.

When Trish's mouth fell open, Danielle knew she'd said too much. "Oh my God, he asked you out?"

She tossed the box on the counter and took her seat. "He invited me to lunch, but I said no. Then he asked me to meet him for a drink that wasn't a date."

"And?"

As much as she tried, Danielle couldn't hold back her grin. "I went." She sipped her wine for courage. "I also paid."

"Cheap bastard." Trish opened the pizza box. "Is this safe for me to eat?"

Danielle laughed. "I didn't make it."

Her friend wiped her brow with the back of her hand. "Whew."

"He's nice. It doesn't hurt that he's really handsome, but you know how I feel. Sleeping with Chris was the worst mistake I made."

"Not true," Trish said over a bite. "Marrying Chris was worse. Sleeping with him was fine." She filled their wine glasses again. "Maybe you should hop on the saddle again. Do you think James would be a good ride?"

"No idea, but I imagine I wouldn't know the difference. Chris was—"

"Lacking?" Trish licked the red sauce off her finger. "You never once complained."

"Why would I? Some was better than none." She showed a measure by putting her thumb against the first joint of her pinkie finger.

"No way. I'm so happy you divorced that little pecker."

Danielle had spent months wallowing in self-pity. She blamed herself for the failure of their relationship. If she'd been prettier. More interesting. Better in bed. But in hindsight, she should have known. Chris talked about nothing but himself and his successes. At the time, she saw that as confidence. He told her he was a catch, and she believed him. Now she knew the truth. Chris could love no one else because he was too in love with himself.

They chatted for the next thirty minutes. When the timer for the cake went off, they stared at the oven.

"You ready?" Danielle asked.

"Almost." Trish opened the bottle of antacids and washed a few down with her wine. "Ready."

Danielle pulled the oven door down with caution. Nothing would jump out. If it was anything like the last time, she was certain it would be dead. That poor cake made its way to the trash can the minute Trish walked out the door, but this one looked better. Better was a loose term. While it wasn't cracked like dried clay, it wasn't right. One side had sunk.

"I'm a failure." She pulled the pans out of the oven and let them drop onto the counter. Whatever fluff they had whooshed out like a popped balloon. What remained resembled thick pancakes.

"Let's taste it before you flog yourself." Trish slid off her stool and took a knife from the drawer.

"Shouldn't we let it cool?"

Trish sliced into the first pan. "No way. Everything tastes better warm. If it's bad now, it will be awful when it's cold." She gave them each a piece. "On the count of three. One. Two. Th—"

"Wait." Danielle reached for two napkins. "Just in case."

"Three," Trish said and shoved the cake into her mouth. "Not awful. Not amazing either, but it's better." She looked at the piece still in Danielle's hand. "You didn't eat yours."

"I'm afraid."

"Just eat it."

She did and had to admit that while it wasn't pretty to look at, it wasn't bad to eat.

"It's hard to taste the chocolate."

Trish reached for the book, but Danielle pulled it away. "You can't look at it."

"Why not?"

"Because I want to do this myself. It's my independence cake."

"If you call it that, then get red, white, and blue sprinkles. What's it really called?"

"Forever Fudge Cake."

"Something is wrong then." She grabbed the bag of chocolate chips. "Are you sure this is the chocolate it called for?"

"No, it asked for Baker's chocolate and that stuff tastes like monkey ass."

Trish laughed. "Now you're an expert?" She put her empty wine-glass in the sink and kissed Danielle's cheek. "I've got to go. Use the Baker's chocolate and stick to level measurements."

"How do you know these things?"

"I married a baker."

"He makes bagels."

"Same thing, but different."

They walked to the front door. "What if it sinks again? I only get one more try before the potluck."

"Make extra frosting."

"Oh no. I forgot about the frosting."

Trish laughed all the way to her car. "Save yourself and everyone else and buy the frosting."

"No way. I want them to eat it and think it's really something."

Trish opened her door and tossed her purse inside. "Oh, they'll think it's something all right."

Danielle watched as the lights to Trish's car disappeared. She hung her head and walked back inside. Currently her cake baking had the same success ratio as her relationships—total failure.

When she entered the kitchen, she took a stool and dragged the book across the counter to read the preface again.

Everything I learned about love, I learned from baking.

"Hogwash." Then again, maybe Adelaide knew something. Men were a lot like cakes. Sometimes they fell flat. Sometimes their emotions were an arid desert. Where was the decadent man of her dreams?

She scraped the cake into the trash can and grabbed the last piece of pizza and the bottle of wine. Thoughts of love made her think of her marriage, and thoughts of Chris made her want to watch an episode of *Murder, She Wrote.*

⸻

SHE STARED at the cake from Connie's Confections with its piped icing and little gold candies decorating the top. She nudged one to the side so it wouldn't look perfect. She hated that she caved and bought the cake but given that she'd failed at wowing her new bosses on day one, she imagined giving them food poisoning wouldn't go over well. She debated for several minutes about moving the cake to a plate now or in the morning. "Nothing like the present." She pulled out her only platter. It was one her mother had given her for a wedding gift. A white scalloped plate that had been passed down through generations. It was supposed be used for happy occasions. It would be perfect for desperation as well.

With the precision of a surgeon, she used a knife to separate the cake from its cardboard base and proceeded to gently slide the masterpiece onto the plate. On the last little shove, the whole thing toppled to the floor. She hadn't realized each time she shifted the cake she was also shifting the plate.

At her feet, in a mountain of chocolate and china shards was her future. She wanted to collapse in the pile and give up but the pile of bills sitting on the edge of the island meant she had to get up and fix it.

She allowed herself five minutes to cry over the plate and another five for the fifty dollars she spent on the cake before she pulled out the ingredients to Adelaide Phelps Forever Fudge Cake.

Hours later, spent emotionally and exhausted physically, she sat on the floor in front of the oven. "Please. Please. Please," she said over and over again as she stared through the oven window to watch the cake bake. This was her last chance to make it perfect. She followed the recipe exactly—okay not exactly. She still couldn't bring herself to use the bar of baking chocolate. Since the recipe asked her to grate it anyway, she substituted cocoa powder in equal measure.

The minutes ticked by as her confidence grew. There were no cracks or obvious problems. When the timer rang, and she pulled the pans from the oven, she held her breath and waited for them to deflate. To her surprise and excitement, they didn't. While one wasn't perfectly level, it was acceptable. Right now, acceptable was a win in her book.

She glanced at the clock, and it was five in the morning. How had she stayed up all night baking? Looking at the three disasters sitting like roadkill on her counter, she knew the hours had been eaten up, because she refused to fail. While she readied herself for work, the cake would cool. She took the frosting she made earlier from the refrigerator so it could soften. While it was grainy, it was edible, and actually tasted like chocolate.

When she entered the shower, she thought about how much her life had changed in the last few weeks. She'd met disaster at every corner and survived. James told her that sometimes change was good. In that moment, she couldn't see anything positive in the changes that were happening everywhere. New management brought its own set of complications, but it also brought progress. There was a time when she was embarrassed to work at The Pines, but now she was filled with a sense of pride. Big things were happening. The lobby was truly luxurious. The rooms were transforming before her eyes. New pool furniture arrived just yesterday, and she could envision their guests sipping pretty colored drinks decorated with fruit and umbrellas.

Though she hated to admit it, James was right. Thinking about James sent her heart racing. Every day he came bearing a cup of coffee, she wanted to reach out and kiss him, but she'd been impulsive and reckless once before, and she couldn't afford to let her guard down again.

"Maybe you should throw caution to the wind," she said out loud. Could her disaster with Chris be a one-off? She shook those thoughts from her head. She didn't have time for what-ifs. There was a cake to frost and a potluck to attend.

Chapter 10

JAMES

Reveals were the best part of his job, and today James tucked himself in the back corner while his sister stood at the front ready to welcome the staff to their new lounge. Normally, he'd be up front with her and Julian, but he was still keeping a low profile.

One by one the department heads filed inside the room. The first to arrive carrying a box of store-bought cookies was Willetta from housekeeping. Next was Paul from security. In his hand was a plate of bagels. James never considered a bagel a dessert, but he imagined it was all perspective. Spread with honey butter or butter and cinnamon sugar and the breakfast item was easily transformed.

Todd arrived with cupcakes, and Flynn carried in a pan of something that smelled like heaven.

Danielle walked in with a cake. By the slightly odd angle it tilted, it appeared homemade. She said she made a mean cake, and this one looked out of sorts. He chuckled to himself at the memory of her dashing out of Halfpipe panicking about the potluck. What was it she said? *Should it be edible, or should she try for something that wouldn't kill anyone?* Maybe she wasn't a baker after all.

"Looks great," he said as she set it on the table at the back of the room.

"It shouldn't send you to the hospital." She looked around the lounge. "This is amazing. You did a great job."

"Thank you." He pointed to the fancy coffee maker. "I got that for you. You want to try it out?"

She beat him to the machine. "Oh, my goodness. This is amazing."

"Let me make your first cup."

"You know how to work it?"

He was at a loss, but not afraid to try. "How hard can it be?"

She rested her hip on the counter and watched him.

"I think the coffee goes here." He lifted a lid and peeked inside.

"You're fired." She moved closer and bumped him out of the way with her hip. "Water goes there."

"How do you know?"

"I have a similar machine at home."

"But you asked if they would hire a barista for the general manager's machine."

She filled the basket with coffee grounds and tamped it down.

"A girl can dream and then beg for access."

The dark roast smell filled the air, and people migrated to the espresso machine. She handed him the first cup. As she made hers, she gave a lesson on how to use the machine.

Her consideration touched James. When the second cup finished, she added copious amounts of sugar, took a drink, and smiled. "Maybe I should stick to coffee."

Allie got the attention of the staff with a loud, high-pitched whistle. James was certain dogs within a mile were howling.

"Good afternoon. Welcome to our new lounge. At Luxe, we believe family comes first. We started renovations on the lounge because having a place to relax and unwind is important. If you love what you see, thank my b …" She looked at him and shook her head. "Thank James. Dig into the food we catered. I know, funny to bring in something when we have the talented Flynn to cook for us, but we wanted to give him a well-deserved break. Enjoy your lunch. We have some exciting announcements to make when everyone is finished. Someone in this room's life is about to change."

Just then, Chris walked in empty-handed. "Were you referring to me? I am a life-changer."

"Got that right," Danielle whispered under her breath.

James raised an eyebrow in question but decided it would be best not to push at the moment.

The scent of savory barbecue sauce filled the air as people piled their plates with chicken, brisket, and spicy sausage.

Allie and Julian moved around to mingle, but he found himself staying near Danielle.

"How long did it take you to perfect that cake?"

"Perfect?" She laughed. "I was going for edible."

"Is it?"

She turned to face him. "Is it what?"

"Edible."

She shrugged. "It's a new recipe. I made two and ate part of one just to make sure no one would die today."

He thought she was joking, but she never cracked a smile.

"Note to self, never let Danielle cook for me."

She gave him a soft slug in the arm. "Hey, I'm a mean microwaver."

He rose and went to the dessert table to slice a piece of her cake and then came back. "Let's see here." He forked a piece. "Can you put 911 on speed dial before I gobble this up?"

"Tell you what. I'll steal the first bite. That way, you know I'm not trying to kill the whole team." She leaned forward and took it from his fork. "Amazing," she said after she swallowed and took a drink of coffee to wash it down.

"Really?"

She shook her head. "No, but if you tasted the ones who came before, you'd think this was Michelin Star worthy." She laughed. "My best friend Trish said it tasted like monkey ass."

"And how does she know?"

"She doesn't." Danielle put her hand on her chin. "Then again, she did do a summer work program at the Denver Zoo."

"You said you could make a mean cake?"

She laughed. "What I meant was that I'm a mean cake maker. It's not a pleasant experience and it makes me crabby."

"Good to know."

He forked another bite and shoved it into his mouth before he changed his mind. It was dry when it hit his tongue, but the flavor was there.

It stuck in his throat, so he washed it down with coffee. "Chocolaty."

"That's a whole story on its own. Did you know that when you make a chocolate cake, you have to use a brick of unsweetened cocoa? It's awful, and I refuse to use it. The first two times I used a bag of chocolate chips."

"How did that turn out?" They were only talking about cake. Bad cake at that, but seeing her grow more animated with each story, made him want to eat the whole miserable mess if it kept her there beside him.

She smiled. "Trish was right. It was primate bottom for sure."

They both busted out in laughter.

They grabbed a plate of food, and stood at the back, watching everyone while they ate. It was a comfortable silence. He loved that they could be together and not have to fill every moment with noise. Sometimes the best times were the quiet times.

Allie broke their peaceful moment with an air splitting whistle to get everyone's attention. His sister could quiet a concert hall with that sound.

"Looks like you all had some time to chat and enjoy lunch. Thanks for bringing the desserts they were ... interesting."

Chris piped in. "Bagels were good. The cake had the texture of sand."

"What did you bring, Mr. Putnam?" Allie asked.

He pointed to himself. "The sweetest treat in here. Me."

Allie shook her head. "I asked everyone to make something because what comes from your kitchen often comes from your heart. That says a lot about a person." She pulled Julian to her side and gave James a brief glance. "We've been paying a lot of attention to the upper management, and we've decided on who will get the general manager position."

Willetta raised her hand. "What criteria did you use?"

"Lots," Allie answered. "We gathered data from past profit-and-loss reports. We interviewed your employees. We filtered through guest comments. We watched."

"Sounds like a popularity contest," Paul grumbled.

Chris stood up. "If that's the case, then I win." He began to walk forward like he was accepting a trophy.

"Take a seat, Mr. Putnam," Julian said. He turned to Allie. "You want to make the announcement, or do you want me to?"

She elbowed him. "I want to do it. You're a numbers guy, and I'm a people person," she teased.

"Our new general manager is none other than our chocolate cake maker, Danielle Morgan."

James expected a round of applause, but the first thing that happened was Chris stood up and yelled. "I'm not working for her."

Allie smiled. "That's up to you, Mr. Putnam. Bring me your resignation letter when you decide."

He stormed out, and Flynn stood up and clapped. "That was a good decision. Danielle is perfect for the job."

James watched the man and wondered if Flynn had a crush on Danielle. The fist of jealousy squeezed his gut.

He looked to see her reaction. Her face paled. Maybe the cake was bad, after all.

"You okay?"

She forced a smile on her face. "Yep."

Allie and Julian walked over. "Congratulations."

"Thank you." She took in two deep breaths. "Can you excuse me for a second?" She rushed out of the room.

"Is she okay?" Allie asked.

"No idea. Let me find out." He raced after her and caught up just as she was ducking under the plastic sheeting to her cubicle. "Wrong office." He gently took her arm and led her to the general manager's space. He bypassed the desk and continued through to the studio.

"I can't be the general manager." She collapsed on the couch and buried her face in her hands.

He sat beside her. "Why not? You're perfect for the position."

"I'm not. There are reasons I shouldn't be in charge. Hell, I can't even bake a cake?"

"You and I both know this had nothing to do with that cake, which would have never gotten you the job."

She looked up. Her eyes were jeweled and ready to spill tears. "Bad, right?"

He shook his head. "No, what it lacked in moisture, it had in grit."

"Grit's a good way to describe it. Chris was right; the texture was like sand."

"Maybe, but the flavor was like heaven." He leaned in and cupped her cheek. "Tell me what's wrong."

"Chris is my ex."

"Ex what?" He thumbed away the tear that ran down her face.

"Ex-husband."

Her confession was like a right hook to his chin. "You're kidding?" He wasn't expecting that. If Chris was the caliber of man she preferred, he had no chance. Chris was egotistical, maniacal, and a classic narcissist. He'd never been or would become any of those things.

"I wish I was. He was the biggest mistake of my life."

His hand slipped from her cheek to her shoulder. "We're all entitled to one. I had a mistake, too. But your past shouldn't dictate your future. If you turn down the position because of him, he comes out the victor. Do you really want to let him win?"

"No. I'd rather give him a case of the clap or a bout with food poisoning."

He laughed. "He did eat your cake."

James lifted her chin so he could see her eyes. Because of the tears they were the color of clover or the finest emerald.

"He pretends to be a team player, so he took a bite. He doesn't usually eat sugar. He loves himself too much to do that to his body."

"Sounds like he didn't love you enough." He pulled her into his arms and held her. All he wanted to do was kiss her, but this moment wasn't about him. It was about her.

She snuggled into his embrace and laid her head on his chest. This was exactly where she belonged. He was in heaven.

Several moments later, she moved away, sat up, and rubbed her face. "I'm not normally such a mess." She drew in a few deep breaths. "Thank you for being with me."

"There's no one I'd rather be with."

His response came naturally. He leaned forward and kissed her forehead. If he'd been thinking, he would have pulled her into his lap and devoured her lips.

"I'm okay now. I know what I need to do. You're right. I'm not giving him a win. He's taken enough from me already." She pulled her shoulders back and put on a smile that didn't quite reach her eyes.

"You ready to face the world?"

"I am." As they walked back to the lounge, she seemed to grow taller with each step. Everyone was still there, eating their second round of dessert. She took her place at the front of the room. "Sorry for my abrupt departure, that announcement came as a shock, and I needed a minute to process everything." She glanced toward him with a silent thank you in her eyes. "We're already a good team, but we'll become better with the support of our new management."

Flynn raised his hand and asked, "Any advice or wisdom to share?"

She let out a burst of laughter. "Yes, don't touch that chocolate cake if you want to live."

Chapter 11

DANIELLE

How silly was it to be nervous about her first day at her new position? It's not like she hadn't been doing the job forever, anyway. The only difference was now others were accountable to her, including Chris.

Allie and Julian had convinced her to take a couple of days off so she could start fresh. That only gave her more time to worry.

She paced back and forth in front of her bed. There were four blazers on her comforter. All of them said something different. The pink meant she was approachable. The white said she was trustworthy. In her mind, the gray was impartial, and the black meant she was all business. Since today would be the tone-setter, she slipped on the black jacket and headed out the door.

Trish was running up the sidewalk with a paper lunch bag in her hand just as she stepped onto the porch.

"What are you doing here?" Danielle turned around and locked her door.

Trish leaned over and caught her breath. "What kind of friend would I be if I didn't support my bestie on her first day of her new job?"

"Thanks. You're the best friend a girl could have." She eyed the bag and saw her name written on it. The e at the end swirled into a heart. "Did you bring me a bagel?"

"Yep, cinnamon and raisin with double cream cheese. Just the way you like it." Trish thrust the bag forward. "Ask your hunky monkey to get the coffee. Do you think he can train Rob on coffee delivery?"

"Oh please, your husband cleans, cooks, and does dishes."

Trish laughed, "And he's got a good bagel."

Danielle walked toward her car. "Stop bragging."

"Yeah, but James probably has a hammer and wields it like a pro."

"I'm not talking about James' hammer; and, before you ask, I haven't seen it. You know how I feel about getting involved with someone at work. It's bad news all the way around." She opened the door and put the bagel bag on the passenger seat. When she spun around, she pulled Trish in for a hug. "Wish me luck."

Trish squeezed her a little more tightly than normal. "You don't need luck. You'll be great." She let go and stepped back. "You better get to work, or you'll be late."

Once Danielle climbed inside her SUV, she rolled down the window. "What if they don't respect me as a boss?" It was her biggest fear. She had no worries about the job; it was the people that frightened the hell out of her.

"You can fire them and start all over." Trish waved. "I'd start with Chris. If he continues to sleep with guests, that will be a huge problem for the company."

"I'll consider the counsel. Have a great day." Trish skipped to her car and took off.

Danielle contemplated her suggestion. Firing Chris wasn't really an option because he'd claim it was personal. Then again, his sleeping with guests wasn't the biggest problem. She'd been going over the inventories for each department while she was "off", and his data didn't add up. She'd need to keep a close eye on him. All the talk about Chris gave her a bellyache, or maybe it was because she hadn't eaten.

Before she backed out of her driveway, she opened the bag and found the bagel and a juice box. She'd start with half the bagel on the way there.

When she saw her designated parking spot in the garage, her chest swelled with pride. It didn't have her name on it, but it said general manager, and that was enough. She pulled into the spot, grabbed her purse, the paper sack, and headed inside. Like Avis, she could have used the private elevator and avoided everyone, but how was that good for business?

"Good morning, Ms. Morgan," Beverly called from the front desk. She started working at the resort just before the takeover and had the most welcoming smile.

Danielle stood taller and walked with purpose to greet her. "Good morning. You can call me Danielle, we're part of the Luxe family. How are things today?"

"Can't complain." She looked skyward. "There's not much activity with the tower closed, but I cleaned and stocked everything. Mr. Patterson complained about the towels again, so I sent him some from the suites since those rooms aren't being used right now."

"Great job. I have to agree with Mr. Patterson. Sandpaper towels are not a luxury, and this is Luxe. I'll talk to Allie about it. Let's see if we can provide quality linens to everyone." She moved toward the elevator and pressed the button for the corporate offices. It was still number thirteen, but now it was a lucky number.

Gone was the blue confetti carpet. Marble tiles replaced it. Where the cubicles once sat, was a large conference room with a twenty-foot table and a wall of computers. It was amazing how much could happen when the construction crews worked around the clock. She'd been gone two days and a week's worth of work was finished. Her heels clicked across the flooring until she reached the lounge.

Inside stood James with his back to her. She'd recognize his behind anywhere. The way those jeans hugged his backside and thighs was almost pornographic. At least it was with her. She'd had many a sleepless night thinking about the power of those thighs since she met him. With a full cup of coffee on the counter next to him and another brewing in the machine, he pulled out the jar of sugar packets and opened a dozen of them.

"Figured it out?"

He spun around to face her. "What? The sugar or you?"

She walked inside and stood beside him. "The machine."

"I did." He handed her a cup of sweet heaven. "For you."

"Why are you always bringing me coffee?"

"You're much more pleasant after your fifth cup."

He leaned against the counter like he belonged there. With one foot crossed over the other, he was the picture of calm. James held a certain air that was both attractive and dangerous for her. She liked men who were self-assured; it was how she ended up with Chris. It wasn't until she was in too deep that she realized Chris's boasting wasn't confidence, but his need to stroke his own ego.

James was different. He didn't brag; he did. His actions spoke louder than any words he could say.

"It's my third."

His shoulders shook with his laugh. "I have to put two more into you before you grace me with your smile then." He pointed to the counter that held several days old desserts from their meeting. "How about a piece of your cake to sweeten you up?" He kicked off the counter and moved to the desserts.

She set her mug down and lunged forward to swipe the cake away before he could slice into it.

"Don't torture yourself." She stared at the paper bag in her hand. There was still a half a bagel and a juice box. "If you're hungry, have this. My best friend's husband owns Abrams bagels." She reached in and took out the half she hadn't eaten and gave it to him.

"You ate the good half."

She always started with the top half because it was fluffier and had more raisins. "I did. Are you saying you don't want what I'm offering?"

He raised a brow. "What would that be?" He closed the distance between them.

"A bagel." She stepped back. There was an inferno building between them, and she could hardly stand the heat.

"Are you sure that's it?" He moved another step toward her, trapping her against the counter. "Just this bagel?"

She opened and closed her mouth several times.

The *clickety-clack* of Allie's heels saved her from saying anything else.

"You ready?" Allie asked as she turned the corner into the lounge.

"Yep," Danielle said, sidestepping James. "Just tossing the cake away." She dumped it in the trash can and placed the plate in the sink for washing later. She picked up her coffee and rushed out the door.

"You made that cake, right?"

"Will it affect my job if I say yes?"

Allie moved ahead of her toward the conference room. "It will only affect you if your sense of humor is as dry as that cake. Next time look up high-altitude baking."

Danielle could have taken offense, but she didn't. The cake was a work in progress. The Mona Lisa wasn't painted in a day. The Parthenon didn't get built in a week. All masterpieces took time. One day she'd make the perfect Forever Fudge Cake. She hoped that it would happen before anyone died from her cooking.

"Questions before the staff arrives?" Allie asked.

This would be Danielle's first meeting as the general manager of the hotel.

"No, let me put my stuff away and grab my notebook. I worked the last two days analyzing the numbers. I wanted to have my facts and figures straight."

"That's why we gave you the job. You're conscientious, but you should have taken the days to relax." Allie looked like she was analyzing her. "Good choice for the meeting. Black means business."

Danielle rushed to her new office to put away her purse and juice box. She picked up the folder containing her notes and headed back to the conference room. On her way, she remembered Beverly's comments about the linens.

She walked in and looked at the table, wondering where her place was. It was as if Allie read her mind.

"You are at the head of the table. I'll sit next to you to be your wing woman."

Danielle placed her folder and her coffee in front of her seat. Her hands shook. Inside her chest, a herd of buffalo trampled her confidence.

She cleared her throat. "What are we going to do about the linens? They're substandard and guests have complained."

Allie sat down and took out her planner. "I'm in negotiations with the supplier, but the man is difficult. We always try to keep things local to support the community." She slapped her hand on the wooden table. "You'd think he'd be more amenable considering the amount of money we're spending to replace everything." She scribbled something on the page and closed it up. "I'm on it." She rolled back and looked at Danielle, "What's wrong with these people. It's not just the linen guy, but the produce people too. You ask for sweet potatoes, and they give you yams. They want to get paid a lot and do very little."

"Working with people can be frustrating." Danielle looked at the clock. It was nine o'clock, and her staff was late. *What if they didn't show?*

As the thought ran through her head, Willetta and Paul arrived with Todd and Flynn right behind. To her surprise, Chris pulled up the tail end.

"Welcome to our first Department Head meeting," Danielle said.

"You have five minutes to get coffee or a soda from the lounge, and then we'll start."

She needed the five minutes to calm her nerves. Maybe three cups of coffee was too much before a meeting. Maybe it wasn't enough.

She watched everyone file out of the room they'd just entered. Moving in the opposite direction of the crowd was James. He smiled and gave her a thumbs-up before mouthing the words, "good luck."

When everyone returned, she stood and addressed the room. She figured it was best to drop the bomb first and then work on cleaning up the mess.

"Soft bonuses have to stop." Her focus was on Chris because he was the biggest offender. "Whether you're giving yourself extra time off or have a great side business selling what you can pilfer, it has to end. As valued members of the Luxe family, you will be compensated fairly. Your salary will be based on performance. Do your job, and you'll get rewarded. Steal from the company, and you're gone." She took a silent breath and waited for someone to defend themselves. No one did.

When her gaze fell on Chris, he shook his head. After a ten-second stare-down, he pushed his chair back from the table and stood.

"I can't work with you."

This was the moment she'd expected and prepared for. He would behave as if she were punishing him. She had to put her feelings aside, but she also had to establish herself as his boss. "You don't work with me. You work for me. There's a difference. Now sit down or leave. If you choose the second option, I'll take that as your resignation."

He flopped back into his chair. His expression was that of a young boy sitting in time-out.

When she turned, Allie smiled with pride.

The meeting continued for another fifteen minutes, where they addressed expectations and concerns. Once finished, they all went to work.

Danielle entered her office, closed the door, and called Trish.

"How's it going?" her friend asked.

"Please tell me this isn't a real juice box but a wine juice box." She stared at the label that showed smiley face grapes.

"I'll come over later with the real stuff. Rob has poker night with the boys. Shall I bring a bottle or a magnum?"

"Does it come in IV bags?"

"A magnum then. First days are tough."

"It went as well as I could expect." In hindsight, it went better. Chris could have thrown an all-out tantrum. Instead, he threw a mini hissy fit.

"Did you call your mom and tell her about your new job and new boyfriend?"

"No, why would I do that?"

"Because she's your mom and mom's love to brag about their kids. Give her something to talk about other than your sisters' happy marriages and their beautiful children." In the background, Trish made gagging sounds.

"If that's your best argument, it's a fail."

"Just call her, she might surprise you." There was a pause. "Florida is two hours ahead, so you'll catch her before she trots off to mahjong, or tai chi, or whatever else retirees do down there."

"It's pinochle or bowling, I think."

"Call her."

"Fine, I will."

Trish hung up, and Danielle stared at her phone. It took her five minutes to press the button that dialed her mother's home.

"Danielle," her mother squealed. "It's been so long since we've heard from you."

Had it been that long? She mentally counted and sighed. The last time she called was for her mother's birthday.

"Sorry Mom, I've been busy."

"Too busy to call your mother?"

She wanted to tell her the phone dialed both ways, but that wasn't wise. "I called to tell you the good news."

"You and Chris reconciled?"

A bit of bile rose in her throat. "No, that will never happen." She'd never told her mother the details because she felt ashamed that she wasn't enough, but maybe now was the right time. "He cheated on me, Mom."

There was a moment of silence. "Oh, honey, I didn't know."

"I didn't tell you because I thought you'd blame me."

"Danielle Morgan, cheating is a character flaw. That's on him and not on you."

"Thanks for that, but honestly, I'm over it. It's in the past." For the first time in a year, she felt free of regret and remorse. "I've got news about my future. I've been promoted to general manager."

"That's wonderful, sweetheart." She laughed. "I was kind of hoping you'd tell me there was a new man."

Some things would never change. Meredith Morgan was from an era that believed life wasn't possible without a man. She thought about James and how good he made her feel.

"There might be someone. It's not anything at this point, but I've met a nice man." She leaned into her chair and relaxed. This was her office. She was moving up in the world. Her new position came with a sizable raise. Things were looking up.

"What's his name and what does he do?"

Typical Mom questions. They were to be expected. She'd need to tell the book club on Friday.

"His name is James, and he's in construction."

"Oh." There was another long pause. "You know, sweetheart. You can do better than that."

She wanted to bang her head against the table. "You know what, Mom? I've learned it's all about the quality of the man, not the size of his bank account, but thanks for the confidence."

"Keep me posted." She heard the jingle of keys. "I've got to go because Ginny Pemberton is hosting pinochle today, and she makes the best snacks. One minute late, and I'll miss out on the cheese rangoons. Love you, honey."

Her mother hung up before she could return the sentiment.

She spun in a circle in her chair and soaked in the beauty of her office with its hardwood shelving and light marble flooring. Things were looking up. Life was good.

Chapter 12

JAMES

His phone buzzed as he exited the elevator on the fifteenth floor. It was his sister summoning him to the twelfth floor to talk about the meeting.

Be there in a minute.

She could wait while he looked over the work done to the suites. They were in decent shape already, so outside of an upgrade to the bathrooms, they'd finish in no time. Next week they would double their construction efforts to get the tower completed early.

As soon as Allie's special-order desk arrived, he could get her off the twelfth floor and begin work there. Julian was the smart one. He worked from home.

He took the stairs down and stood in front of Allie's door.

She opened before he knocked.

"Took you long enough."

"I have work to do, and I'm not your beck and call boy. Don't forget my stake in this venture sits at the same percentage as yours."

She gripped his arm and pulled him inside. "Whatever." She moved to the table and sat. "I wish you had been there. She ran that room like a drill sergeant runs recruits."

"Like you'd know anything about drill sergeants or recruits." While he served his country for one enlistment period, his sister finished her degree in business management at Wharton. He'd never forget how angry his father was when he joined the Army, but James was proud to serve his country. It made him appreciate the cost of freedom. He had the utmost respect for those who wore a uniform.

"I've watched *An Officer and a Gentleman*," she said. "Anyway, she's a sharp one. I think we picked a winner."

"How did everyone else respond to her?" He wished he could have been there, but he wasn't ready to reveal himself.

"Everyone seemed okay, but Chris. We need to do something about him." She kicked off her heels and rubbed her feet.

He never understood why Allie insisted on wearing such tall shoes. Maybe it was because she was petite, and wearing them gave her confidence. They probably gave her bunions and corns, too. Never a day went by that he didn't count his blessing to be born with an X and Y chromosome. Women had it tougher than men in almost every way.

"We need to let Danielle handle Chris." He sat on the edge of one bed. "Did you know he was her ex-husband?"

Allie's jaw dropped. "No way. That guy? He's an arrogant ass."

"Hard to believe, I know."

She chewed on the end of her pen. "Maybe she's not a good fit for the job, after all." She tossed the pen aside and wiped her lips with the back of her hand looking for ink.

"Why would you say that? While Flynn was my first choice, I can see she's perfect." He wanted to pull the last two words back. They were telling and spoke to how he felt about Danielle.

"You don't have to take up a sword for her. All I'm saying is maybe she doesn't have good decision-making skills." She spun her chair to face him. "Chris falls somewhere between primate and Neanderthal."

"Everyone has a type. What's yours, Allie? Don't judge Danielle for making a mistake. I've made one, and you forgave me. Hell, you gave up. That's hardly better."

"We're not talking about me, but let's talk about you." She leaned forward and stared at him. It was her human lie detector look that always did him in. "You like her."

He stood, shoved his hands in his pockets, and walked to the window so she couldn't see his face. "I do. She's part of the Luxe family."

"My bullshit meter is going off." She rose and joined him. Once she got to the window, she tugged on his arm so he had to face her. "Oh my God, you really like her." She poked his chest. "I'm so glad my big brother's heart is thawing."

He swatted at her hand as it came up to poke him again. "My heart wasn't frozen."

"Again, I'm calling bullshit. You were permafrost after the divorce."

"Not true. Besides, you don't get to analyze my behavior with relationships until you've been in one."

"I've been in one."

"Ashley Dunhurst doesn't count. You both had too much to drink at my wedding. It didn't last."

"You're right because he didn't last. He was three strokes and out. He was also a wimp. I can't have a relationship with a man whose penis is smaller than mine. There was also Brandon, but he had a word allergy."

"That's your problem, you intimidate most men."

The carpet muffled the stomp of her bare foot. "I'm five foot three and sweet as cotton candy."

"You're five foot eight in heels, and you might think you're cotton candy, but you have a temper as hot as a ghost pepper."

She wrapped her arms around him and gave him a hug. "I see what you're doing. You're deflecting from talking about your love life." She stepped back. "You don't have to hide from me. We're family, and I'll always have your back."

"I know, and I swear, Grace never calls."

She waved her hand through the air, almost catching him on the side of the head. If she'd connected, he would have to believe it was intentional. Allie was very much like their father. Even with her red hair and hot temper, she wasn't impulsive. She was deliberate about everything she did.

"I'm not talking about Grace. I'm talking about Danielle."

"There's nothing going on with Dani and me." *When did I give her a nickname?*

Allie's brows lifted. "Dani?"

"Short for Danielle. It means nothing."

She went back to her chair and picked up her soda. She deliberately moved slowly. He knew her well. She was taking her time, and that meant she was planning.

"Do you think it's wise to sleep with her?"

"I'm not sleeping with her." He shoved his hands into his pockets and shuffled back and forth.

"But you want to, right?"

She had him there. There was no doubt his slight smile was his tell. "All right. I like her. She's different."

Allie clucked her tongue. "She's also your employee."

"No, she's *your* employee. I'm in charge of construction. I rarely get involved in the business side of things."

"Be careful with that one, she could be trouble for you."

"I'll be cautious. As it is, I'm just her coffee boy."

Allie slipped her shoes back on. "And her confidant, if she told you Chris was her ex. I didn't even know that."

"We're becoming friends. That's all."

"Right." She nodded her head. "You know why women are so good in business?"

He didn't want to know. He needed to get on with his day, but there was no shutting up his little sister. "No, tell me," he said as he walked backward to the door.

She tapped her fingers against her skull. "It's because we think with this head, first."

He gripped the doorknob. "Not true. You think with your heart."

"Okay, but it's better than thinking with our—"

"Gotta go." He opened the door. "What's on your agenda the rest of the day?"

"I'm battling over sheets and bath towels."

"Nothing's worth going to battle over, but love."

"Says the divorced guy."

He stepped out of the room. "To the woman who doesn't date." He was about to close the door but stuck his head back inside. "I've loved and lost, and I want to love again. Maybe she's the one."

Allie blew him a kiss. "I hope so. I really hope so."

Although he should have checked on his various crews, talk of Dani made him miss her. He took the stairs up one floor and walked into the corridor that led to the executive offices. When he got to hers, he heard a man yelling.

"I won't have you punishing me because you were inadequate as a wife."

James recognized Chris's voice and hurried toward the argument.

"I'm not punishing you. You're punishing yourself by not doing the job you were hired for. There's a discrepancy in your inventory. I'd suggest you do another count."

James stood out of the way and listened.

"My inventory is none of your business. It was all right with Avis."

"Avis isn't here. I am, and I'm asking for you to take another look and see why you ordered six dozen fishing rods and reels a month ago, and now you have twenty in stock."

As soon as he heard someone's fist hit the desk like a gavel, he rushed inside.

"Are you ready?"

She straightened her papers and stood. "Yes." She walked to the door and waited for Chris to exit the office. "I'll expect the recount within a week."

Her ex walked away and said, "Don't hold your breath."

She turned to James. "Your timing was perfect. Thanks for the save." She twirled her finger in a strand of hair that fell over her shoulder. "It was a save, right? We didn't have an appointment that I missed, did we?"

He was used to seeing her with her hair tied in a messy bun. Looking at her hair hanging down left him speechless.

"Lunch," he said, shaking himself out of his trance. "We had a lunch date." He gently took her elbow and guided her to the executive elevator. "I think Italian sounds great."

"We didn't have a lunch date. I would have remembered that."

"You're right, but I saved you, and now you owe me. I think lunch is the perfect payback."

She looked over her shoulder. "I shouldn't leave. I've got a lot of work to do."

"You have to eat. A half a bagel won't keep you for long."

She gave him a smile that clenched his heart. "Don't forget. I had the good half."

"That's right. Still, a lunch date sounds perfect."

The elevator door opened. She stopped before she stepped inside. "Wait. I need my wallet."

He pulled her inside and pushed the button for the ground floor. "My treat." He took out his phone and texted his sister.

Taking Dani to lunch. Be back in an hour.

She texted back.

Wielding my sword still, or I'd join you two.

He laughed.

You weren't invited.

He tucked his phone inside his pocket. "Just telling my crew I'll be off-site for a bit."

"Good idea." She pulled her phone from her jacket pocket and did the same. They exited and walked through the garage to the street. One block down was Pasqual's. "This isn't a date."

"You can pretend it's not, but this is definitely a date." He wrapped his arm around her shoulder and tugged her closer.

When the hostess came to the front, he asked for a quiet table in the corner. He pulled her seat out and took the one next to her.

"You want to talk about what I walked into?"

"I don't talk about my ex on a first date, do you?"

He knew his smile was big by how it stretched his cheeks. "Nope, but glad we're on the same page about what this is."

"I'm hungry, and I have no money with me. That puts me in an agreeable mood."

"I might have to keep you hungry and without resources more often."

"Haha." She opened the menu. "What do you recommend?"

"Do you want to be content or fall in love?"

He reached over and set his hand on top of hers. It was the first real intimate moment they'd shared. The day in the studio when he hugged her and kissed her head didn't count because he was in comforting mode, now he was in courting mode.

"Are we talking about the food?"

He gave her hand a squeeze. "If we're discussing the food, I'd go for the lasagna. It's earth-shattering."

"And if we're not?"

"I'd say go for it, too." He let go of her hand and opened his in the air as if mimicking an explosion. "That can be earth-shattering as well."

Her cheeks turned ripe strawberry red. She lifted the menu and hid behind it. "I think I'll have spaghetti and meatballs. I may not be up to earth-shattering at this point."

He lowered the menu. "Are we talking about the food?"

She lifted her chin. "What else would we be talking about?"

"What else, indeed?"

Allie was right. Dani would be trouble, but now he was certain she was the good kind.

Chapter 13

DANIELLE

How late was it? She parked her car and rushed to where Trish sat on the front steps of her craftsman bungalow, holding a bottle of wine in one hand and a lemon Bundt cake in the other.

"You brought two hands of heaven. You're a godsend."

"I believe I am." She rocked back and forth until she gained the momentum to stand. "I come bearing the elixir of the gods and a sinful sweet." She lifted the two gifts in the air. "Devil in one hand ... Angel in the other. Which will it be?"

Danielle unlocked the door and swiped the wine from her friend's hand. "Let's start with the wine and quickly move onto dessert." She tossed her purse and keys on the entry table and walked to the kitchen. "Does it smell like chocolate in here?"

Trish lifted her nose in the air. "Yes, but no surprise there, you've been baking like a maniac. How many cakes did you throw away?"

Danielle took two wineglasses from the cupboard and searched two drawers for the wine opener. When she turned around, Trish was already pouring.

"How did you—"

Trish lifted the bottle opener. "It was on the counter. I swear you're losing your mind."

With her palms against her face, she tried to rub the stress of the day away. "First day exhaustion and exhilaration. Experience one of them and you're okay but deal with both on the same day, and it sucks the energy right from under your skin. Then there's the upcoming training. They're sending me to their resort in Brecken-ridge for a week."

The feet of the stool squeaked against the wooden floor when Trish pulled it away from the island and took her seat. She always chose the one closest to the door for a quick escape.

"Why didn't you request something better, like Rome?"

"We don't have a location in Rome. Breckenridge is perfect. At least I speak their language."

"Very true. Now tell me about your day, dear," her friend teased.

Danielle took the other stool, and after a deep drink, she told Trish about the events leading up to her encounter with Chris.

"I never liked Chris. You finally have an excellent opportunity to prove who you are, and he's going to eff it all up."

As soon as Trish got married, she gave up cursing. She figured it would take her a year to clean up her act, and then she could try for a baby. Her greatest fear was for her child to have its first word be a four-letter expletive.

As her best friend and her baby's unofficial, non-familial aunt, she'd given up cursing as well—mostly. Okay, she cursed like a trucker when she was alone. It was like that saying, if a tree fell in the woods and no one was around to hear it, would it make a sound? If no one heard her curse, then it didn't count.

"How did I not see he was an A-hole and a big D with a little d? He has to brag about his conquests because if he didn't, no one would know he'd scored, including the women he was with. Being married to him was a big yawn."

"He really said you were an inadequate wife?"

"Yes. It was so embarrassing because seconds later, James walked in."

Trish set her glass down and leaned in. "Hold the door. You never mentioned James." She had this uncanny ability to raise a single brow without contorting other features on her face. "James, the hammer wielder?"

Danielle laughed. She'd thought about his hammer several times since she'd met him. She was certain it sat between two hard as anvil thighs to protect it.

"He was passing through and heard the argument."

"Hearing about Chris is like watching a rerun of a show I hate, but this is getting interesting. What did James do?"

Warm fuzzy tendrils of heat coiled in her stomach. "He took me to lunch."

"Oh my God. You could have led with that. You had a date with the hot guy?"

This conversation needed a full glass of wine, so she tipped the bottle over their glasses and topped them off.

"To call it a date would be an exaggeration, but he saved me from an ugly scene. He came into my office like a knight on a white steed and asked me if I was ready."

"Are you ever?" Trish sucked down half her glass with one drink. "If your ex wasn't there, you could have stripped naked and laid on your new desk." She tapped the island. "It's solid enough to hold you both, right?"

"You and your surfaces. I'm surprised you're not black and blue."

"Who says I'm not?" She giggled. "Pass on the tile floor though, those grout lines can be a pain—literally."

Danielle wadded a napkin and tossed it at her friend. "We ate at Pasqual's."

"I love that place. Their lasagna is—"

"Earth-shattering. I know. I've heard."

"You had it then?"

"No, I'm out of practice. It's not wise to jump right into an earthquake. I started with a small tremor. The spaghetti and meatballs were darn amazing, too. I didn't really think of it as a date. Although, he kept saying it was."

"Who paid?"

Danielle lowered her head.

"He did."

"It was a date." She reached over and patted Danielle on the head. "My girl had her first date. I'm so excited."

The problem with Trish was she made a big deal out of nothing. Danielle would rather eat lemon cake than talk about the perfect lunch with James. She reached for the plastic container and pulled off the cover.

Without having to get up, she took a knife from the wooden block sitting on the counter and sliced them both a sizable piece.

"You talk as if I've never had lunch with a man."

Trish shoved a bite of cake into her mouth and tapped her fingers on the granite counter until she finished chewing and swallowing.

"You haven't eaten with a real man in years. James sounds like the real deal. Chris was a boy who flunked man training—a dozen times. What was it you liked about him?"

"His confidence."

"That wasn't confidence." Trish washed her next bite of lemon cake down with a sip of wine. "That was arrogance, and it only works if he can back it up, which he couldn't. That man cheated, not because you were inadequate, but because you proved he was. You were smarter and wiser and out of his league."

"I feel that way about James. He's completely out of mine."

Trish wobbled and nearly fell off her stool. "He's a construction worker."

An unexpected sigh snuck out. "He's so much more than that. I don't know why, but I feel that construction isn't where he peaked in his career, but the work he enjoys the most. He's brilliant. I'm sure we could talk about anything from literature to politics."

"Tell me you didn't talk politics on the first date. That's a serious faux pas."

"No, we didn't, but we could have. There's a confidence about him that makes me believe even if we were at opposite ends of the political spectrum, he'd happily discuss and listen to my opinion."

"Damn." Trish slapped her hand over her mouth. "See what you did? You broke my thirty days without swearing record."

"I didn't put that word in your mouth." She pointed to the cake. "Eat more so you can sweeten your disposition."

"You should go for it with James."

Her head shook back and forth, even though her mind was screaming yes. "I know, but it's not wise. We work together."

"We're back to that? If I followed your line of thinking, I'd be single and still have my old entry table."

"Not the same. You and Rob never worked together."

"Neither do you and James. I sold Rob insurance for his building. That's as far as our work connection went. James will finish the construction on the resort, and he'll move to the next project. Your work relationship ends there."

"You're right." There was some merit to her argument. Danielle had to admit she was gun shy.

"I know. I'm good at being right. I keep reminding Rob of that, but he wants to be right too. I've negotiated that with him. Poker night is his time."

"But he's out with the guys."

A smug smile teased at her lips. "I know. He can be right with them, but when he gets home, it's my turn."

"I don't know how you snagged that man."

Trish sat up. "I told him I was a smart choice. Confidence is sexy when you can back it up." She tapped her chest. "I'm the best thing to happen to Rob. I remind him every day."

Danielle folded over herself until her head rested on the countertop next to the wine and cake. "I don't know what I can offer a man."

"Are you kidding me?" She tugged at Danielle's arm until she sat up. "Let's start with your perfect C cups. Not too little. Not too big. You have a backside that makes men bite their knuckles. I've seen it at least a half dozen times when we went to the club."

"I miss the club. Why did you have to get married? Wasn't I enough to keep you single?"

Trish moved the wine out of the way. "No more wine for you. You're talking crazy now."

"I know, but I miss you and our marathon movie Mondays. What about two-step Tuesdays at the Cowboy Club?"

"You can't two-step."

"You're right, but after a few glasses of wine no one noticed."

Laughter filled the air. "Everyone noticed." She emptied her glass and slid it away. "I miss fondue Fridays, but my behind doesn't. Too much cheese does awful things to a girl's body."

"Nonsense. I bet we have the strongest bones in Timberline."

"If he asks you out again, please say yes. Now I feel guilty for falling in love." Trish opened her arms for a hug.

She fell into Trish's embrace. "Don't feel guilty. I'm happy for you. I really am, but I'm lonely."

When Trish pulled back, she focused on the cake ingredients that perpetually sat on the counter waiting for greatness to happen.

"We've got enough time to make another cake. Although the last one couldn't have been bad since you got the job."

Danielle rose from her stool. "Thankfully, I was judged on effort and not outcome. Even Allie, the new COO, told me it was bad."

"She said that?"

"No, but she pointed out it was dry. Said something about high-altitude cooking."

Trish palmed her forehead. "Why didn't I think about that?" She pulled out her phone. "It says here that you need more liquid. Two tablespoons at 3,000 ft., and an additional 1 1/2 *teaspoons* for every 1,000 ft. beyond that." She whistled. "Liquid can include eggs, water, or milk."

"That's it?"

"No, you must add flour too."

Danielle moved the ingredients to the island and gathered the mixing bowls. "Seems counterproductive."

"Did you use the right chocolate the last time?"

"No, I used cocoa."

Trish opened the cupboard and searched for the bar of Baker's chocolate. "Everything in life is about the ingredients. You put the wrong stuff together, and you get a calamity."

"Like me and Chris."

"Exactly. He's lox, which are amazing if combined with cream cheese and a bagel. You're not a bagel, you're more like a graham cracker. Lox and graham crackers aren't a good mix. What you need is to find your chocolate bar and marshmallows."

Danielle measured out the flour. "Graham crackers are good alone too."

"Better as a s'more."

They worked side by side to put the ingredients together.

"Can you believe I've baked something?"

Trish hip-checked her, sending her stumbling to the side. "Never thought you'd actually take it up as a hobby."

Chocolate flakes went everywhere as Danielle grated the unsweetened chocolate bar. "I only did it to prove you wrong."

"If I said you'd never date James, would you do it to spite me?"

"Probably." She didn't need a reason to be interested in James. She was already there, but if she pretended to date him out of spite, then at least she wouldn't have to take the blame when it went south.

Several minutes later, she finished the batter and preheated the oven. They stuck the pans on the center rack and waited.

"You'll never date James," Trish said to test her theory.

"You're probably right, but that's one time I'd like to prove you wrong."

"Come here." Trish gave her a solid hug. "Wouldn't it be great if he was one of the right ingredients?"

"We're baking a cake, not making love."

Trish looked at her phone. "Speaking of love, Rob will be home soon, and I get to be right. Right in bed when he arrives." She gathered her keys and blew Danielle a kiss. "Text me and let me know if the cake is perfect and take a picture of James. I want to see the face of the man who makes my friend's lady bits twirl."

Danielle walked her to the door. "There is no twirling."

"Yet," Trish yelled back.

"By the way," Danielle yelled after her. "You were right about my mom."

"I know." Trish smiled before she climbed inside her car.

Danielle walked into the kitchen, happier than she could believe. When the timer went off, she took out the cake. It wasn't lopsided and was a deep chocolate color. It smelled great. She glanced at the lemon Bundt on the counter. It was perfect—moist and flavorful. Now she knew why they called it Forever Fudge Cake. It would take forever to perfect.

She didn't bother to make frosting. It was a waste of good butter and her coveted sugar if she couldn't get the cake right. Once cooled, she cut out a sliver and tasted it.

"Not bad, but not perfect." She covered it with plastic wrap and walked into her bedroom.

She stared at the empty bed with its cozy down-filled duvet and wondered how James would look in it.

Chapter 14

JAMES

Could he strangle his sister and get away with it? Sending Dani to an off-site management training program was great, but the timing was all wrong. They had finally gotten past the I-can't-date-you argument at lunch and she hadn't been at the office for a week.

Thankfully, she was due back today, and he wouldn't miss the first chance to see her.

There was no reason for him to be on the executive floor because they had finished the work. He was there waiting with two cups of coffee in his hands when the elevator arrived with her on board.

Her head was down when the door opened, and when she lifted it to step out, she smiled bright enough to light a dim room.

"Were you waiting for me, or was this a coincidence?" She stared at the coffee cups. "Or maybe that's for someone else?"

He pushed the mug forward. "No one else. Only you." She took the cup and walked with him down the hallway toward her office. "I put in three extra sugars in case you weren't feeling all that sweet, considering you've been in training all week."

"How did you know?"

"Allie told me, but I would have rather heard it from you."

"I'm sorry, I would have called or texted, but I don't know how to get a hold of you. She kind of sprung it on me."

Me too. Which was another reason to tighten the noose around his sister's neck.

"I guess the training generally comes later, but the general manager is going on maternity leave."

He wasn't worried about being outed. He imagined his sister picked that location for his benefit since it was the only site he hadn't physically worked at. Luxe at Breckenridgeinridge came about when he was in the army. Julian and Allie had been working without him for the first few years while he finished his service commitment. He created the plans for the remodel but wasn't there to do the work.

He followed her, and the smell of her perfume wafted beneath his nose. "What is that scent you wear?"

She laughed. "It's a mix of fear and intimidation."

"You fear me?"

She put her purse on the desk and sat behind it. Her palms brushed the top of the hardwood surface.

"I'm afraid of everything. My life hasn't been this mixed up since the divorce, and that was over a year ago." She picked up the mug and sipped. "You made it perfect; sweet enough to take the edge off my bitterness."

"Mixed up how?"

She moved her free hand through the air. "Oh, you know ... new job. Crush on you. Knowing one is bad for the other." She stared up at him. "I thought about you a lot."

"I thought about you too." He took a seat in front of her desk. "I think we could be good for each other."

"I can't argue that, but ..." She pointed between them. "This thing churning between us won't be good for my job, and I need my job. I got rid of my ex but got custody of his debt."

He sat up. "How is that possible?"

"You know those pre-approved credit cards that come in the

mail?" She twisted her hands together. "He transferred all his debt to them, and they were solely in my name."

"I so want to kick his ass."

"Me too." She leaned back and closed her eyes. "You'd think it would be marital debt and be split, which would have been a lesser travesty since I don't believe in credit, but we had a judge that decided since we weren't married long, we'd each take the debt in our names and split the debt that wasn't. Lucky for me, Chris has been making the payment on his car by himself."

"Let me guess, it's in both of your names?" He had the urge to rush down to where the asshole hung out and take him to the lake and drown him. Problem was, the guy had such an inflated ego there was no doubt he'd float to the top. "Do you have a house? If so, who got that?"

She raised her hand. "I did. He was happy to sign it over since the debt-to-equity ratio wasn't in our favor."

"That was a good thing. Do you like the house?"

The tenseness in her shoulders released. "I love the house. It's a craftsman style bungalow that has a great cottage feel." It was obvious by her smile that her home brought comfort. "In truth, I picked it out and decorated it. As long as it had a recliner and a television, he was happy. With the house that is."

"He's an idiot."

"Something we can agree on." She pulled out a notepad and rose from her chair. "I need to take a walk around the site. See you later?"

He stood and waited for her to leave her office then walked her to the elevator. "I'll pick you up right here for dinner at six."

"I can't."

He frowned. "Can't or won't?"

The bell to the elevator dinged, and the doors opened. "There's not much difference at this point."

As the doors closed, he said. "I'll be waiting here for you."

An hour later, he was in the basement checking out the upgrades when he heard voices.

"How's the new job?"

He peeked around the corner to see Willetta and Danielle.

"It's good. In truth, not much different from the old job except this one comes with a better office and a few other perks. I came down to see if there was anything I could do to help make your job easier."

"My job is easy. You know why?"

"No idea, but I'd love to hear."

From his vantage point, he saw Willetta lean against the wall. She looked his way, and he pulled back far enough to be out of sight but not out of hearing range.

"I make good choices. I hire people who work hard. Like you, they take pride in what they do."

"Thank you for noticing," Danielle said.

"I do notice. I also notice that handsome construction worker following you around. I think he's got a crush on you."

James wanted to laugh, but that would give up his position. *Is he that obvious about his attraction to Danielle?*

"James is a good man. He's been very helpful to me since I took the position."

"I'm going to give you a good piece of advice. Helpful is another word for sexy. So is kind and considerate. It doesn't hurt that he's handsome, but that's the least appealing part of him. If you think there's magic there, then do something about it. Magic isn't all that common."

"You're right. I could use a little magic in my life."

James could hear the smile in her voice.

"I know I'm right. I've got twenty years of experience on you."

"You don't look a day over twenty-five, Willetta."

He loved the way Dani interacted with others. They always seemed at ease in her presence. Everyone but Chris and he didn't count. Willetta was in late fifties, and while she was youthful looking, she didn't look twenty-five. "Well, that bit of magic is sunscreen and wrinkle cream. Start now, and you won't regret it later."

"Thanks for the advice."

"Anytime. I wouldn't call it advice. It's more of a regurgitation of my thoughts."

"Fair enough. Are you sure there isn't anything I can do for you?"

It impressed him that despite her overwhelming schedule, she reached out to others to make their lives easier.

"I could use higher quality linen. When things go wrong there, housekeeping is always the fall guy."

"Allie is working on that. It's their policy to try to work with existing vendors."

Willetta *pfffted.* "Time to take out the trash with this one. You get what you pay for, and we aren't getting much."

Afraid of being caught eavesdropping, he exited into the stairwell and went back to work. Six o'clock couldn't get there soon enough.

When the end of the day arrived, James went home to change and hurried back so he was waiting by the elevator as promised. He leaned against the far wall and tapped his shoe on the marble flooring. He glanced at his watch several times. At five after six, he almost gave up. His heart felt as heavy as a five-pound bag of sugar. Then the elevator door opened, and she bounded out, pulling her hair from the messy bun she'd worn all day.

"Sorry I'm late. I got caught up visiting most of the department heads and lost track of time."

"You came." He was elated and surprised.

"I'd never leave you waiting. That would be plain rude." She headed for her office at a quick clip—almost a run. "Where are we going?"

"Black Diamond Steakhouse." He'd been there several times and liked the ambiance. It was dark, and the booths were high and secluded, which would give them space away from others to get to know one another.

She moved around the office like a tightly wound toy. "Perfect, I get to pay this time."

He knew her financial situation, and there was no way he'd let her pay for their dinner at one of the most expensive places in town.

"I got it. I like to pay."

She shouldered her purse and walked out the door. "We can argue later. I didn't have time to eat earlier, and I'm hangry."

He chased after her to the elevator. "Do I have to bring you lunch too?"

"Maybe. Let's see how dinner goes."

The restaurant wasn't within walking distance. It sat on the edge of the lake, two miles north of Luxe.

It tempted him to sneak a kiss when he helped her into his truck, but he didn't dare ruin the moment. A kiss might make her nervous. Instead, he leaned over her and helped buckle her in.

As soon as he opened his door, the flash from her phone's camera went off, nearly blinding him.

"You taking my picture?"

She moved her fingers across the screen. "I promised my best friend Trish. Now that she has your picture, she'll know who to hunt down if I come up missing."

"I'm not going to tie you up and kidnap you." He backed out of his parking spot and started their short drive to the lake. "I don't bring the bondage stuff out until the second date." He risked a glance at her and saw she was laughing. "What?"

"It is our second date."

"You're right." He looked behind him to the bed of his truck. "I've got rope if you're really into that."

"I'm not, but I like to see you're prepared for anything."

He raised three fingers. "Like a boy scout."

Their table was waiting when they arrived. He rested his hand on her lower back to guide her to the booth.

Before she could open the menu, he said, "It's my treat. Please don't argue."

He loved it when her frown turned into a pout. Those lips puckered out and begged to be nipped. "I think your hard hat has given you a brain callus. This place is expensive. Why don't we split the bill?"

He shook his head. "Nope, but I promise not to order the 2001 Screaming Eagle from Napa."

She reached for the wine list and scanned it quickly. "That's crazy. Three thousand dollars for wine?"

He shrugged. "Some things are worth whatever they cost."

The sommelier stopped by before she could respond.

"I'll have a glass of the house cab," Dani told him.

"No, she won't. Bring us a bottle of the Pride Reserve Cabernet."

The man left, and James scooted close enough for their knees to touch. "This is a special night. It deserves a good wine."

She trailed her finger down the wine list. "But it's two hundred dollars."

He pushed the wine list away and covered her hand with his. "Dani, I do okay. You don't have to worry about my bank account." He loved that she was there with him because of him, not his net worth.

"You called me Dani. My grandfather used to call me that. He sang "Danny Boy" to me but changed it to Dani girl."

"I hope it's okay." He reached up and brushed her hair from her face. "You seem like a Dani to me."

She leaned into his hand. "Yes, it's okay. I like it."

"I like you." He was just about to kiss her when the wine showed up.

The sommelier poured a splash into a glass, and James swirled it around and took a sip. When he nodded his head in approval, they were each poured a serving.

When the waiter left, he picked up his glass. "To Dani, who said yes when she wanted to say no."

She picked up hers. "To James, who makes it hard to say no."

They touched glasses and took their first sip.

Her eyes grew wide. "Oh my. This is good. It's so smooth and velvety on my tongue."

He laughed. "If you like this, you'd love the Screaming Eagle. Shall I call him back and order a bottle?"

She gasped. "No. Have you really tasted it?"

He didn't like to bring up his past on a date, but he knew a lot about her, and she had very little information about him.

He took a deeper drink before he began. "I was married once. We had a bottle for our wedding." He didn't want to tell her they served the wine to all their guests that day.

"Very nice gift." She ran her finger around the rim of her glass. "Sorry your marriage didn't work out."

"I'd say the same for you, but I'm glad it didn't, or you wouldn't be sitting here with me."

She picked up her glass and raised it. "Here's to despicable partners." Once the words were out, she cringed. "Sorry, was she despicable?"

He was falling for her. He loved her independence, and innocence, and her wit and wisdom. "The worst kind ever. She had an affair."

Dani held his hand. "I'm so sorry. That's the worst betrayal ever. Chris did the same. To make matters worse, it was with a hotel guest."

His whole body turned to stone.

"How did you find out?" Chris had to go. He was bad for business and bad for Dani.

"There was a noise complaint on the third floor. I knocked, but no one answered. I entered with my key to make sure everyone was okay." She covered her eyes with her hand. "No one should have to see that. The rest is history."

He knew Dani had to deal with Chris herself, and he'd let her until it became too much, and then he'd step in.

"You are worth so much more than he gave you."

"That's what my friend Trish says."

"I already like her."

She pulled out her phone. "She thinks you're," she traced her finger down her screen. "Here it is. You're 'a tablespoon of temptation.'"

"Is that so? Is that all she said?" He knew there was more because, from his seat, he could see the text, and it went on and on.

"No." She turned red like the wine. "But that's all I'm telling you."

He looked toward her phone. "I can see from here it says my lips look like kissable pillows. My arms look strong enough to hold you while I swing my hammer for hours. Care to explain?"

"No." She flagged the waiter over to order dinner. "I told you I'm famished."

"You told me you were hangry."

"You've been warned."

"I can take it. Don't forget ..." He flexed his arm. "I got these and a hammer to defend myself."

She wiped her brow as if she'd broken into a sweat. "I need more wine."

"You'll be fine."

"So, how are the Broncos doing?"

He laughed at her not-so-subtle change of subject.

"Not really a sports fan."

"Did you grow up here?"

He shook his head. "I grew up in a lot of places, here being one of them, but moved to the opposite coast to study architecture at Cornell. After I graduated, I did four years in the army, and the rest is history."

"Cornell? You must owe a bundle in student loans." She touched the bottle of wine. "Are we going to dine and dash? I have heels on which might slow me down."

The laugh rose up from deep inside him until he couldn't contain it. "Dine and dash? Not my style. I told you, I do okay."

"Are your parents rich?"

Rich was an understatement. "They're comfortable."

When their meals came, they ate and talked throughout dinner.

She didn't pump him for more information about his family, which was refreshing. She asked if he had siblings, and he said one but didn't elaborate, and she didn't press.

He asked about her family and found out she was the oldest of three daughters and the only one that failed at marriage. Her parents lived in Florida and recently celebrated their fortieth anniversary with a cruise to the Caribbean.

When the bill came, she reached for it, but he was faster.

"How about a walk near the lake?"

"Sounds fabulous." She held on to his arm and rested her head on his shoulder. "This might be the best date of my life."

"You've had a dull life, Dani. How about we put a little excitement in it?"

He paid the bill, and they left.

"What do you do for fun?"

He wrapped his arm around her shoulders and led her toward the end of a nearby dock.

"This is fun."

"So, you date a lot?" She turned her face to look at him, and all he could see were unanswered questions in her eyes. "Do you bring many women here?"

He recognized the look. It was one that begged him not to hurt her.

"No one but you. I promise you're the only one." That rang true in his heart. How was it possible to fall for a woman he hadn't so much as kissed? All night her lips called to him.

When they reached the end, he turned her around to face him. His hands slid up her arms to her shoulders. He held her there for a moment and looked into her eyes. The moon danced in her irises.

One hand left her shoulder to cup her jaw, and the pad of his thumb traced her lower lip. Even in the moonlight, he could see it quiver as if she were struggling to hold something back.

"I've dreamed of kissing your lips. Fantasized about how soft they were."

She stepped closer, the tips of her breasts grazing his chest. The hitch of her breath making restraint almost impossible.

"What will your mouth taste like Dani? Will it be tart like the wine you drank or sweet like the sugar you pour into your coffee?" His hand moved from her jawline to the nape of her neck. "Are you a taker, or will you give in equal measure?" He leaned in until he was a breath away. The heat of her exhale warmed his lips. "Those lips have been torturing me for weeks."

He bent over and pressed his mouth to hers. It was an innocent first kiss until he moved closer, crushing his chest to hers. He angled his head, and when she opened her lips for him, it got real, extremely fast.

Every fantasy he had paled in comparison to the reality. She tasted like everything from wine and sugar to passion.

Her arms wrapped around his waist and held him tight. He wasn't going anywhere. He wanted more—so much more from her. He nipped her lower lip, and she squeaked but continued to kiss him with wild abandon. She gave as much as she took. He nipped. She nibbled. He pushed. She pressed. He moved. She moaned. For every one of his actions, she had an equally passionate reaction.

The kiss deepened. As his tongue stroked hers, he felt the connection deep inside. It was as if Dani Morgan held a string, and with one pull, she could unravel the knots in his heart.

He hoped that this kiss, their first kiss, was the one she'd been waiting for her whole life.

When she collapsed into him, trusting that he'd catch her and keep her safe, he knew he'd accomplished what the kiss set out to do. He had weakened her knees and her resolve.

When he pulled away, she glowed under the moonlight. There was a light in her eyes and blush to her cheeks he'd never seen.

"Wow, that was ..." She dropped her forehead to his chest.

"That was perfect, Dani. Just perfect."

She sighed. "It was a perfect way to end the evening."

He knew she was right. They needed to go, but he didn't want to. "I should get you back since we both have work tomorrow."

She pulled away and took her phone from her pocket. "How did it get so late?"

"Good wine, good food, and an amazing date. Add a fifteen-minute kiss at the end, and I'd say we had a great night."

He led her to the truck and helped her inside. When he climbed behind the wheel, he asked, "What about the weekend? I can take you anywhere you want to go."

She reached for his hand and held it while he drove out of the parking lot. "How about a night in? Pizza and a movie at my place?"

"Are you cooking?"

"No, I'll order delivery."

"Then I'll come."

She let go and gave him a gentle punch to the arm. "You're awful."

"Dani, I'm good." He grabbed her hand and brought it to his lips. "Really good."

Chapter 15

DANIELLE

The feel of his kiss never left her lips. No matter where she was in the hotel, whether it was in the kitchen tasting the new specials or in the bowels of the hotel looking at the updated electrical panels, he was there with her.

"Danielle, did you hear me?" Todd asked.

"What?" She shook her head. "I'm sorry. You were saying the new equipment was a godsend, and the back-up generator was long overdue."

He chuckled. "That was two minutes ago. I was just saying the new owners are great, and I can't wait to see what will happen with the place." He tapped another piece of equipment. "This bad boy will ensure the guests have hot water for years to come."

"I'm glad you're pleased. Allie assures me every department will get what they need." She looked down at the clipboard in her hand. She wouldn't ask everyone this question, because in her mind only two people besides her could run the resort. "Are you disappointed you didn't get the job as general manager? You would have made a great one."

He shook his head. "No, you're perfect for the position. I'm not a people person, which is why engineering suits me well. I'm more analytical than social. Had they chosen me, I would have questioned their intelligence."

"Don't think I haven't. I'm not sure I'm the right choice either, but I'll make sure I do my best, and that means everyone will be taken care of."

He walked her to the door. "That's why they chose you."

She smiled and took the elevator up. It stopped one floor up, and James walked in.

Every cell in her body woke up. "Are you stalking me?" he asked.

"What? Of course not."

At the next floor, the elevator stopped again, and one of his crew members got on. James moved closer to her. His hand skimmed hers until the next stop when his man left, and another entered.

"Got the tiles laid today," the man said. "Love that granite Allie picked out."

"Beautiful," James replied, but something told her he wasn't talking to the worker. As they made their way up to another floor, he moved his hand to her back, where he drew circles up and down her spine. Every cell in her being tingled.

"Where are you headed?" he whispered.

"Fifth floor to see Willetta. What about you?" Although there was a man standing in front of them, they were alone. Just the two of them sharing a private bubble.

"I'm heading to ten unless you need me for anything?"

She leaned into him. "Nope, I'm good."

The door opened, and the other man left. She waited for someone else to enter, but no one did. When the door closed, he moved fast, pressing her against the wall and kissing her. The air left her lungs. The man made her breathless.

When he pulled away. He smiled. "I've been craving that kiss all day."

"Me too." She giggled like a schoolgirl.

"Any chance you can get away for lunch? I know this great little studio apartment behind your office."

"I wish, but I've got lots of work to finish before my hot date tonight. I don't want to be late."

"Hot huh?"

The elevator door opened, and she stepped out. "Sizzling," she said before it closed again.

She walked down the hallway with a canyon wide smile pasted to her face.

Willetta exited an empty room. "Look at that smile," she said. "You better be here to tell me you had a date with James."

"I did, and it was amazing."

"Kisses like a god, huh?"

She touched her mouth, certain the evidence of their last kiss was on her lips. "No." She looked around to make sure no one was listening. "He kisses like a porn star."

Willetta gave her a pat on the back. "You deserve good things."

That was something she'd been hearing a lot lately and was finally believing. She did deserve good things, and James was one of them.

They talked about linen and new spa products going into the rooms before she continued her rounds.

Next was security. Paul sat behind a desk of cameras drinking a diet soda. "I heard you were making the rounds." Each time he talked his chin wobbled. "The new system is amazing. I don't have to leave my seat to figure out what's happening anywhere in the hotel."

She leaned against the table. "You may not have to leave your station for your job, but you should for your health."

He kicked his chair back and struggled to stand. "Now you sound like my doctor."

Paul had been around long before she was. It was hard to tell his age, but she'd put him somewhere near his late fifties. "I care about your health."

He gathered his things and set them on the end of the table.

"Then you'll be happy to know I've started walking to work. It's only a mile, but it's a start." He patted his belly. "Time to lose the tire."

That surprised her. "Wow, that's awesome. Was that a suggestion from your doctor?"

He laughed, and his jowls shook. "He's been suggesting exercise for a decade, but I figured if the resort was getting an upgrade, I needed to do the same for myself. Besides, there's a cutie working the gift shop that I'd like to ask on a date when I drop ten pounds."

"Good for you." At the mention of a date, she panicked. How did the time get away from her? She had a date at her house with James in less than an hour. She hadn't had a man in her house since she booted Chris out. She'd cleaned and dusted that morning, but who knew how much had settled again. First impressions were important.

"I've got to go. Have a good weekend." She rushed to her office to grab her purse.

"Do you have a minute?" Allie called from the conference room. On the large table were towels and sheets and tablecloths and napkins.

Danielle didn't have a minute, but how could she say no to her boss? "Sure."

Allie picked up a towel and tossed it to Danielle. "Would you want to dry off with that?"

She ran her hands on what should have been cotton-soft and plush. It was more like rough sandpaper. "If I wanted to exfoliate."

"Exactly." She pushed the sheet across the table. "Sleeping on this would be like going to a summer camp where they use two hundred thread count sheets." She threw her hands in the air. "This is Luxe, and there's nothing luxurious about these."

"Do you want me to call the distributor?"

She cackled like a madwoman. "Oh no, it's useless. He's in Europe for the next three weeks, and his assistant is incompetent. He's probably vacationing with the produce guy because he's unreachable too."

Time was moving too quickly. Another fifteen minutes were

gone, and she needed to go. "Let me know if there's anything I can do for you. I'd be happy to step in and take care of it."

"No, I've got this one. It might be time to pull out my black suit."

"While you prepare for battle, I've got to go." She held up her cell phone. "I'm a phone call away if you need me."

Before Allie could say anything else, she took off to the elevator at a near sprint. As she entered her car, her phone rang.

It was Trish. "Are you excited?" Her friend shouted into the phone.

"Yes, and deaf. What do you want?" She backed out and nearly hit another car.

She could hear the whir of a mixer and knew Trish was at the bagel shop waiting for Rob. "Just to wish you luck and make sure you shaved and trimmed in case ... you know."

Her legs were as smooth as a baby's butt, and she'd made sure the lady bits were nicely groomed too. She had no idea where the night would lead them. If it led to bed, at least her sheets were nicer than Luxe's. There were few things she splurged on, but sheets and wrinkle cream were two of them.

"How was your week? Did you sneak off to private places to touch and feel with your construction stud? Get it? Construction ... stud ... nailed you. I'm full of wit and wisdom today."

"You're full of something."

"So ... I need details."

She sighed. "Not much to tell. The week was busy. I hardly saw him at all except for a kiss I stole in the studio apartment behind my office." She dragged him in on the guise that the coffee maker didn't work. After another electrical kiss, she raced to meet Allie downstairs in the lobby to talk about hiring someone for her old job. "And the one he stole in the elevator this afternoon."

"That's not good. You'll have to up your game to make sure he stays into you."

"He hasn't been in me." She turned at the light and pushed the speed limit to her house. "We snuck a kiss in the stairwell, too, but it was quick because there were some teenagers sucking face on the landing above us."

"How'd that make you feel?"

"Downright naughty. It was like I was a kid again." The excitement of new love had that effect on most people. Even Paul was willing to walk to work to get a date with Marla. She never saw her as the cutie he did, but the notion that love was alive at Luxe warmed her.

"Are you making the cake?"

She pulled into her driveway and rushed to her door. "No way, I don't want to kill the man."

"It's getting better each time you bake one."

"How would you know? You didn't stick around to taste it."

"No, but I came by today and dropped off a gift, and the half-eaten cake was still on your counter."

Danielle dropped her keys and her purse on the entry table and rushed to the kitchen, where she found a jar of body chocolate. "I should take your key away."

"Or use my gift. You decide which appeals to you more."

"I've got to go. He'll be here in less than ten minutes." She hung up and looked around the kitchen. With one swipe, the cake went into the trash can. She picked up the body chocolate and tucked it inside the cupboard. There was no time to fantasize about chocolate and James' body.

She stripped off her clothes as she moved down the hallway and shoved them into the hamper. Wearing her sexiest bra and panties, she stood in front of her closet, pondering the perfect outfit. Did she go casual and wear yoga pants and a T-shirt, or did she fancy it up and wear a maxi-dress and sandals?

When the doorbell rang, she was out of time. She put on the multicolored dress and slid into her sandals.

On her way to the door, she yanked her elastic tie out and combed through her hair with her fingers. She stopped at the door to take a big breath and put on a smile. Just the thought of him made her grin like a fool.

She swung open the door and standing before her was perfection in jeans carrying a six-pack of beer, a pizza, and a DVD.

"Come on in." She moved to the side so he could enter. Her heart galloped in her chest. She felt like an octogenarian at high altitude without her oxygen tank.

He leaned in to kiss her. It was short and sweet but wonderful. "I've been wanting to do that since the last one."

"Me too, only I thought it would last longer. Given our marathon first kiss, we set the bar high."

He followed her into the kitchen and put their dinner and entertainment down. Before she could take her next breath, his mouth was on hers.

The kiss was slow and sensual. His lips pressed against hers as if he had all the time in the world.

When she opened for him, the gentle sweep of his tongue tasted like peppermint and passion. His hands moved up her back to her neck. It was a gentle grip that kept her exactly where he wanted her.

As he stepped closer, pinning her between the counter and him, she could feel the heat radiate from his body. He was hot and sexy, and for at least that moment, hers.

She melted into him the same way she had at the lake. Only this time, there was no risk of her sinking to the tile floor of her kitchen because she had no room to move. She was good and trapped, and for the first time in a very long time, happy.

How a man could kiss for minutes and not step away a slobbery mess, was a mystery, but James was an oral master. *Is his skill all-inclusive of everything oral?* A giggle bubbled up inside of her that she did her best to hold back.

He broke the kiss and raised a sexy brow. "What's so funny?"

She wanted to slap herself upside the head for ruining the moment. Their kiss had ended because her mind floated to places she hadn't been for well over a year.

"Nothing, I'm just giddy with happiness."

"You're easy to please."

She turned around to face the island. Her back pressed against him; his arousal pressing into her back side. If she'd had time to eat lunch, she would have skipped the pizza and went back to the kisses to see where they would end.

Skipping pizza didn't seem like such a bad idea until her stomach grumbled. It wasn't the soft rumbling of a tummy that needed a little something. It was more like the roar of a gut that hadn't been fed in days.

"Skip lunch again?"

She leaned back and rested her head against his shoulder. "I lost track of time." The sound started again, which made James step to her side and open the pizza box. "Meat lovers with extra mushrooms."

"How did you know I loved mushrooms?"

"You ordered a side of them at the steakhouse." He pulled a beer from the cardboard holder. "I know you prefer wine, but this comes from a local brewer, and it pairs well with what we're having."

Her eyes went to the plain DVD case which didn't divulge the secrets inside.

"You brought a movie?" She moved around the island to get two plates.

"It's a date. I figured dinner and a movie. That is if you have a DVD player. If not, then we'll figure something else out." He put a slice of pizza on each plate and pulled cheese and red pepper packets from his pockets.

She laughed. "Those are some magical jeans. There's always a big surprise waiting inside."

He lifted a brow. "Have you been peeking?" he teased.

The heat of embarrassment rose to her cheeks. While she'd felt the big surprise pressing against her only minutes ago, she hadn't meant her statement to come out sounding sexual.

She couldn't help looking down. When she saw the outline of his endowment, the heat dropped from her face to throb in her core.

"Stop teasing me, and let's eat." She picked up her plate and the beer he'd opened for her and moved toward the living room. "Bring the movie. I have a DVD player and running water."

"Imagine that." He chuckled as he followed her. "Your place is great. I love how homey it feels."

They sat on her overstuffed sofa and put their plates on the coffee table.

Homey was a safe word to use when describing someone's house. Did he really like it, or was he just being nice?

"What are we watching?" She reached for the movie, but he pulled it away and hid it behind his back.

"Guess?"

She could name at least a dozen movies that a guy would watch. "Terminator."

He shook his head. "On a date night? Not likely. Although, I like the movie."

"Can I have a hint?"

He picked up his beer and took a long leisurely drink. Everything he did was measured and unhurried.

Her mind went back to the gutter. Was he a long, leisurely lover as well?

"It's an oldie but a goodie. A cult classic."

It baffled her. Oldies brought movies like Casablanca or Gone with the Wind to her mind. "The Princess Bride?"

He pulled the case from behind his back. "I want this to be a perfect date night. You, me, pizza, beer, and *Sixteen Candles*."

If he hadn't penetrated her fortress protected heart by then, he'd have full access now.

She threw herself into his arms and kissed him. It was quick but thorough because they had pizza to eat and a movie to watch.

"I can't believe you brought this movie. It's ... my favorite."

He set his hands on her hips. "Glad I chose wisely. It was that or *Alien*."

She moved off his lap. "This will get you another kiss, but *Alien* ... that wouldn't have been pretty."

She took the movie and put it in the player then came back to sit beside him. They ate their pizza, drank their beer, and watched Molly Ringwald fall in love. When the movie ended, James helped her tidy up the kitchen.

They were back where the night began. She was in his arms, and he was kissing the life out of her. Or maybe putting it back in her since she'd felt dead inside for so long.

Just as she considered taking the body chocolate from the cupboard, he pulled away.

"I hate for tonight to end, but I have to be at the site early in the morning."

Disappointment weighed about a thousand pounds and sat heavily on her heart. "That's okay. I understand." Work was work, and since eating a good meal and sleeping inside were two things she enjoyed, a paycheck was necessary.

She walked him to the door.

"How about a repeat tomorrow night, only I'll cook for you," he said.

"You brought the pizza, why don't I cook for you?"

He gave her a look that said you-can't-be-serious.

"Okay, you cook for me," she amended. "At your place?"

"Can we do it here? I'm in a temporary situation."

She wondered what that meant. He made enough to afford a place. Maybe he had a roommate. "Sure, my place is perfect."

He looked around her. "It really is perfect." He leaned in and brushed his lips across hers. "I think you're perfect too."

She held the door open while he climbed inside his truck and left. She watched until the glow of his taillights disappeared.

Chapter 16

JAMES

"Did you stay here all night?" he asked Allie when she opened the door to room 1215.

"I did. This is cozier than Dad's house and closer to work." She marched over to the spare queen bed, picked up a towel, and held it in front of her face. "Do you see me? I can see you." She rolled it into a ball and tossed it into the trash can. "That's the crap they're using."

"For now. Everything is changing for the better." How true that statement rang in his heart and head. He wanted to stay longer with Dani the night before, but because of her ex's appalling behavior, it was important for her to know that he was there because he wanted to be with her more than he wanted sex. If the sex was as good as the kisses, then he'd hit the mother lode.

"How was the date?"

His cheeks heated, and he knew he'd blushed like a teenage girl. "It was amazing. She's really something."

Allie moved to the dresser and leaned over it to wipe the makeup smudges from under eyes. "You're going about it all the wrong way. No relationship lasts when it's built on misrepresentation."

"Doling out relationship advice again? How did the last few times you dated turn out?"

"You know how well they went. The last one showed up with a Christmas list that started with a Porsche and ended with an island. I get why you don't want her to know, but eventually, she'll find out."

The Parks' name was synonymous with wealth. "It would be different if I was homeless and pretending to be a millionaire."

"It's no different to a woman. Omission is the same as a lie."

"But my lie only hides the fact that I can afford an eight-figure lifestyle."

Allie stood straight which meant, without heels, she was about five-foot-three.

"You need to tell her the truth if you want this relationship to work." She slid on her heels and grew at least four inches. "I like her, and I think she's good for you. She makes you happy. Don't screw that up."

"I think she might be the one. We all get a do-over. I made a mistake with Grace by working too hard and leaving too much. I won't make the same one with Dani."

"It's so sweet that you're already at the cutesy nickname phase." She shrugged on her jacket. "If I didn't love you so much, I might hate you."

"You'll find your prince." He ducked away from the wadded up towel she used as a projectile and left.

People everywhere considered money a blessing, and it was. He didn't have to worry about his next meal or if he'd go home to a dark house because the electricity payment was late. That was a benefit, but money was also a curse. Having a lot of it meant he had to question people's motives. Were they into him because of who he was or how much he was worth?

He knew that wasn't the case with Dani. She offered to pay for their dates because she worried about his finances. They could dine out every night, and it would be a rounding error in his checkbook.

Tonight, he was cooking her dinner because Dani wasn't pretentious. She didn't expect caviar and Cristal. She just wanted him.

———

WITH THREE BAGS in his arms that contained everything he hoped he'd need, including an indoor grill, he tapped the door with the toe of his shoe.

Seconds later, Dani answered, looking edible in shorts and a T-shirt. He'd never gotten a good look at her legs, but they were remarkable.

She took one look at the load he was carrying and gasped. "Are we feeding an army?"

He stepped inside and headed toward the kitchen.

"No, but I brought enough to make two meals in case I messed up the first one." He set the bags on the island counter. "If I get lost in your kisses, I might burn the first round of steaks."

She bounced on her bare feet. "We're having steak again?"

He forgot they'd been to a steakhouse on their second date. "Wow, I wasn't thinking." He unpacked the ribeyes. "You put these in the freezer for another time, and I'll run out and get chicken or something else."

"You will not. I love steak." She helped unpack the rest of the groceries. "I don't think my house has ever seen this much food."

"What we don't use we can eat another day."

She moved close to him and lifted on her tiptoes for a kiss. "You're confident I'll say yes to another date?"

He pulled out the George Foreman. "I'm cooking, that's got to get me bonus points."

She rocked her head back and forth. "Depends on if you cook a steak like I bake a cake."

"I'm up for the challenge." He lifted the grill and inspected it like it was a science project. "Not sure how this works, but Betty at your local store told me to get one. She said it would change my life."

There were a few scratches on the top and a groove where the drip tray burned. "She sold you this?" Dani cocked her head. "It's used."

"I know, and it only cost me seven dollars at the thrift store. I guess Betty shops there all the time and knows what's in stock."

"She's a sweet woman."

"That she is. If this doesn't work, I'll pan fry these big boys unless you have a barbecue."

She raised both hands in surrender. "Non-cook here. I have a crockpot, though. My mom gave it to me when I was in college."

"Throw it away. It's ancient and the wires could be bad," he teased. "You might burn down the house."

"No worries there, I'm insured. Trish, my best friend, is my agent, so I'm certain she'd hook me up."

He washed his hands and opened the steak packages. After spicing them up, he googled the grill.

"What do you want me to do?" Dani asked.

"Wash the potatoes and stick them in the microwave."

She picked up the large bakers and went to the sink. "I'm a professional microwaver, so you picked the right girl for the job."

"Yes, I did." He meant that in more ways than one. He washed the grill's cook plates and reassembled everything. "These will cook quickly, once it preheats."

She placed the potatoes in the microwave and started them. "How long do we have?"

He pointed to the George Foreman. "When it beeps, we're good to go."

"Perfect." She wrapped her arms around his neck and pulled him down. "It's time for a kiss."

Oh, what a kiss it was. He knew he should have worn his looser fitting jeans because Dani had a way of making him react like a pimply-faced kid getting his first feel.

He'd never had a toe-curling kiss until her. Each time their lips met, he said a silent thanks to her ex for being an idiot.

The timer beeped, telling them the preheating finished, but she held on and kissed him a minute longer. When the microwave beeped, she let go.

"I've got quite an appetite tonight," she said.

"Me too, but it's got very little to do with the steak." He walked by her and gave her bottom a squeeze as if he did it all the time. It felt so natural to walk by and touch her, and yet, he never had. "Where are the plates?"

She pointed to the cupboard to the left of the sink. When he opened it, he found a surprise on the bottom shelf. He turned around and held up the jar of body chocolate.

"Do you have plans for this later?" He grabbed two plates but didn't let go of the jar even though she tried to pluck it from his hand. He loved it when she blushed. All the heat rose to her chest and face. "Glad you thought ahead. I forgot about dessert. Now we're set."

"Give me that."

He shook his head. "Not on your life, sweetheart." He opened the cupboard and put it on the highest shelf, where he knew she'd need a step stool to reach it.

"The sooner we eat, the sooner we get to dessert."

She immediately wrapped her arms around her chest, but not before he saw she was aroused. Thin cotton T-shirts never hid much; how he loved them.

He put the steaks on the grill and closed the lid. The next five minutes would be the longest of his life. Not because of the steaks but what waited for him after. He watched her as she prepared the potatoes, filling them with butter and sour cream and cheese.

He considered how he'd prepare her. Would he start at the top of her and work his way down, or start at the bottom and make his way up? It didn't really matter because he planned to spend most of his time right there in the center.

"I don't see you as a man who shops in the thrift store." She folded the napkins and gathered silverware.

"I've never been in one, but it's amazing what people get rid of.

They had a ton of bikes, and the book section was enormous. A person could spend days walking down the aisles." He opened the lid even though it said not to, but he wanted to make sure everything cooked correctly. Brown grill lines were already forming.

"I get to the flea market most Saturdays with Trish. It's kind of the same, but you get to negotiate the price."

"Did you go today?"

"No, I cleaned the house since you were coming over."

He leaned over and gave her a quick peck on the lips. "You should have gone. I didn't come over tonight to see your house." He took her in from her pink painted toes to her dark coffee-colored hair. "With you in those shorts, I'm not seeing anything but those legs." He squatted in front of her and traced his fingers from her calves to the hem of her shorts. He was tempted to sneak a hand below the fabric, but the timer went off.

He popped up and moved the steaks from the grill to the plates.

"Follow me." Dani said in a low, smoky whisper.

"I'll follow you anywhere." She led him to a table on her back porch. When he saw a bottle of wine opened and breathing, he palmed his forehead. "I forgot about wine."

"That's okay. We make a good team." She poured while he took a seat. "This isn't Screaming Eagle or Pride Reserve, but it's a decent cheap wine you can pretend you like because it's in my budget."

He sipped the Pinot Noir and let it coat his tongue. "It's good. Really good."

"Shall we toast?" she asked.

He lifted his glass. "Here's to steak dinners and body chocolate."

She choked on her wine. "If you must know, Trish brought that over yesterday and left it on my counter. She was afraid I'd feed you my cake, and the night would be over."

"I like the way she thinks. Someday I'll thank her for her inge-nuity and good taste in desserts."

"You can do that if you want to go to the flea market tomorrow.

She and Rob are looking for another lamp, and since I didn't go with her today, I said I'd go and try to find them."

"Sounds great. You said, 'another lamp' like this is a perpetual problem for them."

She swallowed her bite of steak. "First, the steak is amazing. Second, the lamp is an ongoing thing. They're newlyweds, and they do what newlyweds do. They break stuff with all their surface sex." She took another bite.

"Hmmm, surface sex." He gripped the edge of the wrought-iron table and shook it. "Seems sturdy enough."

"No way, you haven't even gotten to second base yet. I'm not having sex for the first time with you on a patio table."

He finished his potato. "Oh, sweetheart. I've been everywhere with you in my mind. This table is tame when it comes to my fantasies."

She nearly fell off her seat. "God, you make me so—"

"Hot?" He pushed out of his chair and stood in front of her. "Say no now, or I'm picking you up and carrying you to bed."

She looked at the table with half-empty plates. "What about the dishes?"

He held out his hand. "Yes or no, Dani. I'm hoping for the former, but I'll accept the latter."

She took his hand and stood. "Yes."

He could feel her tremble and wondered if it was in anticipation or fear. "You have nothing to fear."

She swallowed hard. "I've never slept with a man on the fourth date."

He bent over and swept her into his arms. "I'm worth the wait," he teased.

"What if you don't like me afterward?"

"Impossible." He moved through the kitchen down the hallway. "Is this your room?"

She nodded.

He held her close. His conversation with his sister poked him like a sharp needle. He should have told her who he was by now, but he loved that she wanted him for who she believed him to be.

"Dani, can I ask you a question?"

"I'm on the pill and haven't been sexually active for well over a year," she blurted out.

He pulled her closer and kissed the top of her head. "That's not what I was going to ask." Once he set her on the bed, he knelt before her, looking into her soulful eyes. "Would you care if I was something else?"

"Like what?" Her fingers combed through his hair. "A janitor?"

"Like anything besides what I am." He looked into her eyes and was certain he could see heaven.

"No. I wouldn't care."

Since he was on his knees, he began at the bottom and worked his way up. Smooth calves to firm thighs, his tongue tasted every inch of her. When he got to the hem of her shorts, he didn't want to move his hands from her silky skin, so he tugged at the button and zipper with his teeth.

She helped him by shimmying out of them. He moved up, leaving her in the prettiest pink lace panties. Her T-shirt rose until he couldn't shift it up her body anymore. He tugged it off, leaving her in nothing but silk undergarments.

Making love to Dani wasn't something he'd rush through. He wanted to savor every moment, so he started at the top and moved his way down, spending a lifetime on her breasts. Tasting. Tugging. Teasing. When she quivered beneath his touch, he moved on. After his second pass, she was naked, panting and squirming, and he was ready.

When he pulled away with his lips glistening with her arousal and the taste of her climax on his tongue, she lifted on shaky elbows. "That was amazing."

He didn't expect to push her over the edge so soon, but she was a powder keg ready to explode.

"It only gets better." He gripped the hem of his shirt and pulled it over his head.

"You are so right." She sat up and reached for him, her hands exploring his chest. A single finger traced his body from his breastbone to the trail of hair that disappeared beneath his jeans.

He popped the button, kicked off his shoes, and dropped his pants. All that stood between them was a pair of cotton briefs. When her hand slipped inside to grip him, not even that counted.

His knees went weak, and he fell to the bed. It was her turn to explore, and she was thorough. The way she touched him made him think she was memorizing every hill and valley.

"You're so beautiful," she said.

"I'm okay with that as long as you don't stop touching me." He rolled over and took the top, so his arms bracketed her shoulders, and his length hung heavily between her welcoming thighs.

"I never want to stop touching you." To prove her point, she skimmed her palms over his chest again. "How am I supposed to get any work done when I know this,"—she lowered her hand and gripped him—"is just around the corner?"

He leaned down and kissed her. He hoped the kiss said it all. He wasn't a caveman, but he wanted to pound his chest and claim her. He knew she was the one. She stirred feelings in him that had been dormant for years. Words like forever and marriage and babies didn't sound scary when he thought of Dani. *Did she want those things too?* They had so much to talk about, but tonight wasn't about words.

"I brought a condom." He stared down at her waiting for her reaction.

"You thought it was a sure thing, huh?" Her hands gripped his hips as she moved beneath him.

The corners of his lips lifted into a smile. "I was hopeful."

She laughed as she held him tighter. "You only brought one?"

"One inside the house, I didn't want to seem overconfident. I have a super saver box on the front seat of my truck. I'm happy to wear one, but you should know I've never gone without. Never. You do something to me that makes me want to break my rules."

Her thighs fell open, and she tugged his hips forward. Inch by inch he worked his way to bliss.

"Damn it," he groaned.

She stiffened beneath him. "What? Did I do something wrong?"

"Dani, you did everything right. I'm ruined for all other women."

She relaxed, and a smile as bright as the north star lit up her face. "Be careful with my heart, James. I could fall for you."

He pushed deep inside her. "Baby, you're already behind because I fell for you weeks ago."

"But we only met weeks ago."

He moved inside her. "That's when I tumbled."

He was relentless in the pace and pressure. Her entire body shook as her climax approached. When he finished making love to her, he wanted her to melt into the sheets from exhaustion. He knew when she was close because tiny tremors pulsed against him. Her core tightened like a velvet fist before she exploded around him. He'd never felt anything like it. Sex had always been good, but it had never been like this. Tonight was life-changing. It wouldn't take much to fall completely in love with Dani Morgan. He was more than halfway there already.

Chapter 17

DANIELLE

The morning sun peeked through the curtain to spotlight the half-empty jar of chocolate. Trish knew her desserts.

Danielle laid on her side and watched James sleep. He was exhausted from the workout they had the night before.

Never in her life had anyone done the things he did to her. Every muscle in her body ached from pleasure. She wanted to reach out and touch him to make sure this wasn't a dream—that the beautiful man in front of her was real.

"I can hear you thinking," he whispered. The slow burn of his voice moved through her.

She inched closer and wrapped a leg over his hip. "Not thinking, just admiring."

He opened his eyes, and she fell into their depths. The rich brown with speckles of gold dust and topaz pulled her deeper.

"You're beautiful. Everything about you," he said.

"Are you trying to flatter me to get in my pants?"

He set his palm on her hip and tugged her closer. Close enough to feel his morning arousal against her. "You're not wearing any pants."

"You're right." Never had she felt so comfortable asking for what she wanted, but with James, everything was different. He made it all so easy. "Care to have a quickie?"

He rolled over, so he was on top of her and nuzzled into her neck. "I don't do quick."

"But we have to be at the flea market soon."

He ran his tongue over her collarbone. His touch was electric.

"We're going to be late."

AN HOUR AND A HALF LATER, they paid a dollar to enter the flea market and walked hand-in-hand down the first aisle of vendors.

"The name of the game here is to negotiate the best deal for you and the vendor," she said. "They mark their prices up because they know you'll offer less."

He gave her a peck on the cheek. "Let the negotiating begin." He moved toward the first booth and looked over the trinkets until he found a heart-shaped box. They priced it at five dollars. That seemed to be the standard cost of things.

"How much will you take for this?" He held up the box and opened the lid to show a red velvet interior.

Funny because it was the same box Danielle picked up weeks ago. At that time, she had wondered if her own heart would always be so empty, and now, she knew the answer was no. Her heart surged with feelings for James. She wouldn't call it love, but it was close. How could a woman not love a man who made her feel the way he did? Every cell in her body called out for him.

The vendor looked down at her dog, a mutt with scraggly fur and a snaggle tooth. "I'll take five dollars."

James pulled a ten from his wallet and handed it to the older woman. "I'll give you ten."

"But I only asked for five," she told him.

He tucked the box into Danielle's hand and said, "Sometimes we get more than we asked for." He wrapped his arm around her shoulder and moved toward the next booth. "Take care of my heart, okay?"

In that second, she fell head over heels in love with him.

"You're a poor negotiator."

He shook his head. "How can you put a price on a heart?"

They made their way down the first aisle until they reached the vendor who sold cross-stitch.

"Before you came along, early bedtimes and television were my life."

"Glad I arrived in time to save you."

"You didn't save me from cookbooks." She pulled him toward the table and picked up a book about pickling.

"Why cooking?" He took a step back. "Obviously, the books will come in handy, but most people choose a hobby they'll enjoy."

"It was books or cats, but now ... it's you."

"You're far too pretty and interesting to be a woman with a dozen cats. Besides, I'm a dog person. If we ever get a pet, I'm voting for a chocolate lab."

He talked of them getting a dog like this was a forever deal. Her heart skipped a beat, hoping he was right.

"Did you have a pet as a child?"

He chuckled. "We got a Boston terrier when my parents divorced."

"That's so sad."

He shrugged. "I was grown, and my dad was lonely. He named him Alimony to remind him of the cost of love."

"I get it. I've been paying for my mistake since the day I said I do."

They moved down the row. "I paid for mine with one big check, haven't heard from her in years. It's too bad more marriages don't last."

"Some do. My parents have been married forever." She tucked the heart box he'd purchased into her pocket so she'd have a free hand to pick up other things. There was no way she was letting James go. He was a keeper. "When I say forever, I mean it. They grew up together. Dad's mom was best friends with my Mom's mom. My parents shared a playpen every day while their moms shared coffee."

"Have you thought about having children?"

"I definitely want kids, but I don't want to have them alone. You?"

He stopped and looked at her. "I definitely want kids. I can see them now. They'd have your eyes and your hair." He palmed her cheek. "Your skin and your heart. Or my heart since you have it in your pocket."

Her ovaries cartwheeled. *Is he talking about their kids?*

"As long as we're playing, I think your eyes and hair would be better." She ruffled her fingers through his thick waves. "I also think they need your patience and coffee making skills."

"I'm not playing, Dani. Our children will be amazing."

He was seriously talking about having kids with her. This was a forever kind of relationship. She froze where she stood. Was she getting a second chance at love? After the first disaster, she hadn't considered the possibility because the fallout was too painful. Then again, she thought about the last few weeks and how James had chipped at the ice surrounding her heart. It was fully thawed and warm again.

A thought occurred to her. Maybe it was the *Recipes for Love Cookbook*. She had picked Forever Fudge Cake.

He tugged her over to a table with games, boxes of Legos, and Lincoln Logs. His inner child came out when he reached for the Erector Set.

"I had one of these as a kid." He ran his hand over the box. "I've always loved to build. The other parts of the business aren't my thing. I never got into the numbers game or the operations."

"You'd be great at them all." She handed the vendor a ten-dollar bill and put the Erector Set in his hands.

"I don't need an Erector Set."

"I saw the light of excitement in your eyes. You definitely need it."

"I need you." He set the box on the table and pulled her in for a kiss.

"I run a PG table. Move it along," the vendor said.

James picked up his new toy, and they turned the corner to walk down another aisle.

Danielle laid her head on his arm as they passed table after table of stuff they didn't need. In that moment, the world could fade away, and she wouldn't care. As long as James was at her side, everything would be perfect.

"Since we're getting to know each other better, what would you consider the most important thing in a relationship?" she asked.

He didn't answer immediately. She liked that. Whatever he would say would not be an off-the-cuff response but something thoughtful and from his heart.

"Trust. Without it, you have nothing. What about you?"

She considered a lot of things like patience and kindness. Forgiveness and humility. Resourcefulness, perseverance, and teamwork. She sounded like the cookbook. When it came down to it, James was right.

"Trust is the foundation on which we build everything."

A squeal made her lift her head in time to see Trish rush toward them. She opened her arms wide and plowed straight ahead on a crash course for a hug.

"Brace yourself," Danielle warned.

James held his Erector Set to his chest like armor.

The impact jarred them, but they held their ground because two were stronger than one.

"You made it," Trish said.

James cocked his head. "You must be Trish."

She stood back with her hands on her hips and hummed out an mm mm mm. "You're the hottie with the hammer." She turned to Danielle. "Has he swung it for you?"

"I'll pretend you didn't ask that." Dani waved Rob over. "Can you control your wife?"

He threw his hands in the air. "Nope. She's who she is, and I love her for it." He tugged Trish to his side and kissed her on the head. "Authenticity is hard to find these days."

James shifted the box to his left hand and shook Rob's. "Nice to me you. I'm Dani's boyfriend, James."

Could a woman climax on words alone? He'd claimed her right there in the third aisle of the flea market in front of her best friend.

"Nice to meet you," Rob said. He pointed to Danielle. "Be good to her, or my wife will hurt you or burn down your house."

Danielle laughed. "I'd say he's joking, but it's probably true. Best thing to do is buy insurance from her. She'll never want to pay the claim, so you're probably safer."

James nodded. "I'll keep that in mind when I get a place."

Trish's eyes lit up. She dug through her purse until she found what she was looking for. "If you're in the market for a house, call my uncle Ezra. He'll treat you right." She handed the card to James.

"He split the commission on my house. Three percent can be a lot depending on the price," Danielle said.

"I'll keep that in mind." His stomach growled. "I'm sorry about that. All I've had to eat since dinner was toast and a half jar of chocolate."

He knew exactly what he was doing because he looked from Trish to her and back again.

"Best dessert ever," Trish said with a giggle. She hip-checked Danielle. "You dirty girl."

Rob held up his hand. "Wait a minute. Did you give them our last jar?"

Danielle knew her friend far too well to be embarrassed. "It was six ounces of dark chocolate that took a fifteen-minute shower to wash off."

Trish made a *pffft* sound and waved a hand at her. "You're not supposed to shower it off. You're supposed to lick it off."

James laughed. "When we finished, I was nearing a diabetic coma."

Rob broke in. "So that's a yes? We have no more good-time chocolate?"

Trish lifted on tiptoes and kissed him. "Don't be silly, there's a case coming tomorrow." She looked at Danielle. "For both of us. I love prime shipping."

"A case? What are we going to do with a case?"

James pulled her to his side. "Don't you worry, sweetheart. You're not the only one with a sweet tooth."

Trish's attention went beyond them. "That's the one." She pointed to a lamp on a table ahead. "Nice to meet you, James." Looking at Danielle, she said, "We'll talk later." She tugged Rob's hand, and they left.

"I like them." His expression turned serious. "Rob's right. Authenticity is hard to find."

"So is good food," she said. "I know a great hot dog stand near the park. We can grab one and nap on the lawn when we're finished."

"I've never napped in a park. I'm happy to try it, but if we nap at your house, we can finish that jar of chocolate."

They walked out of the flea market and climbed into his truck.

"You're right. I've got frozen pizza or peanut butter and jelly."

Chapter 18

JAMES

Allie was right. The furniture in the offices was the perfect scale for the space. James stood inside what would be his office. He chose this one because it was directly across from Dani's.

"This looks great." Dani snuck up on him, which was a hard task to pull off since she wore heels every day to work and the cadence of her walk stuck in his brain. She was a *tip-tap tip-tap* person whereas his sister had a *clickety-clack-clunk* kind of walk.

He pulled her into his arms for a kiss and a hug. "I missed you this morning." He'd left her place late last night and went back to his father's cold empty house. It was a long, lonely evening.

"I missed you too, but we can't do this here." She wiggled from his hold. "Someone might see us."

"Does it matter?" he asked. "Are you embarrassed to be my girlfriend?"

She stepped so close their chests touched. "In what universe would it embarrass me to be yours?"

He palmed her hips and tugged her closer. "No one will care what we do." He nuzzled the curve of her neck. "We could break in this new desk." He reached around and knocked on the wood.

"No, we can't. You don't even know whose desk this is. As tempting as your offer sounds, this is my job, and I can't risk it."

"What if this was my office?"

"The question is irrelevant because it's not your office. What if it's Allie's or Julian's, and I have to sit in here for a meeting? I'd never hear a word they said because I'd be thinking about what we did on that desk."

Resignation came in a hearty huff. "How about lunch then? I'll pick up salads from Daisy's." He winked. "We can try out the studio apartment."

She looked around before she pressed a chaste kiss to his lips and stepped away. "Lunch sounds great. Until then, I'm interviewing people for my old job." She looked at her watch. "I've got to go, but can we meet in my office at noon?"

"Your office sounds perfect." He glanced across the hallway and regretted putting in a wall of glass. At the time, he thought it would open up the place, but now he realized she'd get no privacy, which meant they'd get none. The studio was the best thing about this floor outside of Dani.

His phone buzzed. He had reminders scheduled for his meetings. "I'm off to the recreation department. By week's end, I'll have a crew tearing the place apart." They walked out of the room.

"Don't kill him," she teased.

"What if I just hurt him a little?" If only that was an option. The more he heard about Chris, the more he wanted to introduce a fist to his face, but James was a gentleman and he was a professional. There was no need to hurt Chris because if given enough rope, the man would hang himself.

"That also sounds appealing, but I don't want to visit you in jail. Not up for the no-contact clause or the body cavity checks."

"Now, that sounds interesting to me." At the elevator, he gave her another quick kiss. She turned around and walked to the conference room while he went to visit her ex.

Since the outdoor recreation department was on the other side of

the resort near the lake, Chris wasn't under anyone's constant super-
vision. Somehow the security system never seemed to function on
that part of the property.

"Hey, Chris."

Chris nodded toward James before he shoved the rest of a donut
into his mouth. "What brings you out here?" he said around a
mouthful of food.

He pointed to the box tucked under his arm that he picked up on
his way. "New security cameras and I wanted to let you know that
we'll be remodeling next week."

Chris turned around and looked at the shelves haphazardly
stacked with everything from fishing gear to ice skates.

"I've got a system. They shouldn't mess with something that's
working."

Nothing was working in the outdoor recreation department,
including Chris. "I hear the boss lady wants a comprehensive inventory. I figured you could count everything while you move it into
temporary storage."

"The boss lady"—he air quoted—"can want whatever she wants,
but it doesn't mean she'll get it."

"Sounds like you don't like her."

"Like her? Not so much anymore. Hell, I stayed married to her
faithfully for a few weeks. That was actually a record for me. If she
hadn't caught me, I'd still be her husband. She couldn't cook worth a
damn, but she sure could—"

James turned and walked away before the idiot said another
word. They were both lucky because he would risk going to jail for a
chance at one good hit.

He checked in with the various crews working on-site and then
headed to Daisy's to get their lunch. On the way back, he picked up
coffee.

The closer he got to the resort, the quicker his heart beat. She did
that to him. It beat harder and faster today knowing that he would

come clean. They were a breath away from saying I-love-you, and she was entitled to know who he really was.

More than once, he'd slipped about his life and his family. He'd done what he intended to do, and that was get into the building to see how things ran. He got to know everyone without the formality of being an owner of Luxe.

The first few builds they did, he remained anonymous. It was never his intent to be sneaky or dishonest. He was the silent behind-the-scenes partner. People were real with him and didn't feed him what they thought he wanted to hear. They told the truth. Like Rob said yesterday, authenticity was a rare quality. Too bad he had to be inauthentic to get others to be genuine.

The problem with the plan this time was he didn't expect to fall in love. Love complicated everything, and his undercover boss scenario would not last for long. He had to tell her.

When the elevator arrived on the corporate floor, he walked past the conference room. Dani was sitting with a woman. He could see by her body language that she liked the interviewee. She'd let her shoulders fall into their natural relaxed position, and the smile on her face was sincere.

He held up the bag and the coffee and nodded toward her office. She raised her hand, showing she'd be five minutes.

He took the subordinate seat in front of the desk and waited and waited and waited. He had a one o'clock appointment with his sister to talk about the next remodel project. They worked on the things that mattered most to their guests. Polls showed visitors rated the rooms least important as long as they were clean, comfortable, and relatively updated. It was the amenities the resort provided that spoke to their clientele. The pool, the spa, and the outdoor recreation options were huge, along with food and beverage—especially beverage. He had no worries about Flynn. In fact, he was his first choice for general manager, but Allie pointed out that promoting him would put the quality of the food at risk. Flynn ran a tight kitchen, with little turnover and few complaints.

Somehow his sister was usually right. Regarding Dani, she was probably right too. He planned to sell Dani on the benefits of him being an owner. He hoped to convince her that he was the same man. In his eyes, he was, but would he be in hers?

At fifteen minutes to one, she rushed in. "I'm so sorry. She had so many questions."

He'd used the time to make the meal special for her. He'd laid it all out and folded her paper napkin into a swan. He'd doctored her coffee so it was mostly sugar with a touch of caffeine.

"Good interview, then?" He forked a bite of his salad.

"Yes, I have a couple more, but she's at the top of the list."

He swallowed his bite. "That's great. What qualities are most important to you in an employee?"

She consumed her salad like she hadn't eaten all day and knowing Dani she probably hadn't.

"Honesty for sure. I think it's important to surround yourself with people who aren't afraid to tell it like it is. I don't want to hear things are perfect and then find out there's something huge lurking under the surface that I don't know about."

"Some surprises are good."

"Some, but most are just surprises, and the nature of a surprise is that it catches you unaware. I'm not a fan."

He took a couple of deep breaths. "I have something important to tell you." He opened his mouth to blurt it out when his phone buzzed, telling him he had a meeting. "But it will have to wait until later. I've got a meeting I need to get to." He dumped his remaining salad into her trash can. "I really need to talk to you later, okay?"

She dropped her fork. "Are you breaking up with me?"

He chuckled. "Nope, it's something else."

"Terminal illness?"

He shook his head. "Nope."

"You're moving."

He bent over and brushed his lips across hers. "Nothing like that. Let's have dinner out, and I'll tell you."

She exhaled a held breath and smiled. "Dinner sounds good."

"I'll be on twelve if you need me." He left her office feeling hopeful. Dani was a logical thinker. Once he told her his reasoning, she'd understand and be okay with it.

When he got to room 1215, he didn't knock because he had a key. Through the door, he could hear his sister on the phone, and she wasn't happy.

He let himself in quietly, not wanting to disturb her call.

"Unbelievable," she said. When she turned around and saw him standing there, her hands flew in the air along with her phone and coffee. The phone landed on the bed, the coffee on her chest. The dark roast bled into her white silk blouse.

"Why do you do that? Don't sneak up on people." She stared down at her shirt. "You're lucky I buy my favorites in bulk." She marched past him, grabbed the robe from the closet, and shut herself in the bathroom. The water ran for a few minutes, and she grumbled for a few more. She reappeared wrapped in the terry-cloth robe. "Got most of it out, but now I'll have to stay until it dries or call Willetta and see if she can help a girl out."

"First world problems. Stop complaining about a coffee stain when there are people who don't have coffee."

She fisted her hips. "Don't talk to me about privileged problems."

"As for coffee spills, between you and Dani, I'm two for two." He walked to the desk where she'd laid out the architectural plans he'd drawn up for the spa. "I snuck up on her once too."

Her face softened, and a smile lifted her lips. Allie looked so much like their mother it was uncanny.

"How are things going with Dani?"

"Allie," he got breathless thinking about her. "She's the one. I'm hopelessly in love with her. She's sweet and considerate. She puts her all into everything, even if it's a failure."

"Don't worry, I'm not asking her to bake my birthday cake."

"We'll have Flynn make yours. You want it several tiers with pretty flowers and candied pearls?"

"It's going to be my birthday, not my wedding." Picking up a highlighter, she stared down at the plans and drew a circle around the treatment rooms. "Besides, you've got a few months to prepare."

Allie had a big bash yearly. She didn't believe in limiting herself to milestone birthdays. Every year deserved a party.

"What's wrong with the treatment rooms?"

"We need to lose one to expand the others. No one wants a massage in the closet." She drew over the plans with a pink high-lighter. "Like this." She turned to look at him. "Speaking of keeping things in the closet, when are you going to tell her who you really are? The longer you wait, the harder it will be for both of you."

His stomach twisted. "I would have told her at lunch if she weren't running late from an interview, and you weren't waiting for me." He glanced at the plans. "I'll get them redrawn tonight. Right now, I have to out myself to Dani. You're right, the longer I wait, the messier it gets."

She walked him to the door.

As he stepped away, she reached out, fisted his shirt, and yanked him back. "Between all your other commitments, we don't get to see each other enough." She tugged him closer and kissed his cheek. "I love you." He cupped her face like he did Dani's, only this time the gesture was full of brotherly love. "I love you too."

When he turned to leave, he found Dani there. "Is this what you needed to tell me?" She spun around and walked into the nearby stairwell. He could hear her heels on the concrete stairs. Her steps were no longer a light *tip-tap*, but a *boom, boom, boom* like a grenade launcher on rapid-fire.

"Oh hell, I need to talk to her."

Allie stopped him from moving. "No way. Give her a minute to think and to calm down. Going after her now will get you killed."

"If I wait, she'll have more time to believe exactly what she believes. That you and I ..." He shook his head. "Gross."

"Give me one second. Don't go anywhere." She rushed into the room and came back seconds later fastening the last button of her wet shirt. "I'll go talk to her."

He rushed toward the elevator because Allie would never take the stairs. "The truth can't come from you. It has to come from me."

She waited minutes for the car, then entered and pressed the 13th floor. "Fine, I won't tell her anything other than you're not my lover." She shook her head. "Yuck."

Chapter 19

DANIELLE

Back in her office, Danielle paced the floor. She thought her heart hurt when she caught Chris cheating on her, but somehow this was worse because James knew her wound and picked at the scab, anyway. He was the worst sort of man.

"You're so stupid." She saw the cup of coffee he had brought her at lunch sitting on the desk. She picked it up and flung it at the wall. It ran down the beige paint like the tears running down her cheeks. Streaks of hurt and sadness and betrayal.

After five laps around her desk, she flopped into her chair and moved the mouse to wake up her computer. She had no choice about her next move.

"I have to quit." She lowered her head to the hard surface. "What the hell am I going to do?"

She needed to talk to someone, but the person she wanted to speak to was Allie, and she was the problem. Calling Trish would give her a shoulder to cry on, but once the tears were gone, she'd end up with another visit to Aunt Freida. Why was it that people blissfully in love thought everyone should be? Love was like a sweater. To some, it was warm and soft and fuzzy, and to others, it itched and irritated, but to Danielle, there didn't seem to be the perfect feel or fit.

"You should have known," she chastised herself. "Rules protect people." She lifted her hand and pounded her fists on the top of the desk. "Don't date someone in the workplace."

She stared at her hand. "Maybe a big ugly tattoo will work." She picked up her pen and wrote— "Don't be an idiot. Work is for work" —on her hand.

She pulled up a blank page. Work was for work she thought, but now there wouldn't be a job. Not at Luxe anyway. How was she supposed to work for a woman who was sleeping with her boyfriend? "Ex-boyfriend," she reminded herself. She'd lost everything. Somehow losing James seemed worse than losing her job. She could find another job, but he'd crawled into her heart and changed everything. Losing Chris didn't hurt past the betrayal because he brought little to the marriage. James brought so much, and the void would hollow her out.

She looked at the blank screen and started the letter as one would,

Dear Ms. Parks,

She immediately erased that and typed,

Dear Hussy,

She wanted to call her a scumbag whore, but that might take it too far considering James appeared a willing accomplice with his cheek cupping I love you. How many times did a girl have to have sex with him to earn those words? Somewhere deep inside, she wanted them. Kind of like a trophy of some sort.

She backspaced until the page was clean.

To Whom It May Concern:

~~Due to recent~~

~~In light of~~

How did she resign from her job when all she felt was murderous rage?

She began again. Short and to the point.

To Whom It May Concern:
I QUIT!!!!!!
Not so sincerely,
Danielle Morgan

She sent the page to the printer, scribbled her signature on the bottom, and was searching for an envelope when Allie walked in.

Danielle ignored her or at least tried to, but Allie was hard to ignore with her red hair. Then there was the wet shirt that looked remarkably similar to her wall.

The coffee stains didn't go unnoticed by Allie either. "I see you've added an artistic touch." She walked over and touched the still damp wall.

Danielle found a box of envelopes in the side drawer. She fought with the fold to make it fit and gave up. Instead, she bent it any which way and shoved it into the envelope.

She wanted to ball it up and throw it at Allie's pretty face. Shove it down her wet shirt and give her a third boob. Maybe force feed her the first cake she'd ever made, but she couldn't because until she handed her that letter, she was still on Luxe's payroll and still working for the woman in front of her.

"I want to explain," Allie began.

Tossing her hands in the air, Danielle dropped the envelope to the table. "You don't need to explain." She lowered her hands and slid it across the table.

Allie pushed it back. "If this is your resignation letter, I'm not accepting it. What you saw is not what you think you saw."

"I know what I saw. I saw the man I love give himself to someone else."

"You love him?"

Seeing Allie smile made Danielle want to hurt her worse. It was a good thing her pen had rolled off the table, or she would have used it as a weapon. Death by Bic wouldn't be pleasant.

"I did, but I don't share, and I've found most men aren't worth fighting for."

"James is."

Danielle growled, which sounded more like the clearing of the throat of a flu patient. "I won't fight you for him. He's all yours."

Allie moved around the desk to stand beside her. "You and I need to talk. One thing you need to know right now is I've never slept with James, nor would I sleep with him." She made a face like she'd tasted something bad. "Let's grab some coffee and cake, and I'll explain what I can."

"I threw away the cake in the lounge."

"I wasn't talking about that cake. We need good cake. Let's hit Pikes Perk and chat." She looked at her shirt and pointed to an unmarred section. "Besides, I've missed a spot."

Danielle didn't know what to think. Allie wasn't behaving like someone caught doing something despicable. She was trying to talk to her as if she were a friend. Someone like Trish, who would listen for hours and formulate a plan.

"I'll go as long as your aunt isn't a matchmaker, and you don't plan to make me her next client."

Allie cocked her head. "Nope, my aunt is a movie star. She lives in Malibu and is on her fourth husband. Some women have all the luck."

"Some have none." Danielle would put herself in the latter column. She'd also put Allie's aunt there too, but then again, was four times lucky? She imagined it was all perspective.

They walked down the hallway. When they turned the corner to get to the elevator, James was standing there.

Danielle held up her hand. "Not now."

He ignored her request. "Please listen to me. It's not what you think."

She walked past him. "I need a minute or thirty." She wanted to run back and pound on his chest and throw herself into his arms, but she needed information. Information only Allie could give her because desperate men said anything to get back into bed.

She followed her to Pikes Perk, and Allie ordered two Americanos. One decaffeinated with nonfat milk and nonfat vanilla syrup. For the second, she told the barista to fill it with a third cup sugar and then add the coffee.

"How did you know?"

"My b—James has picked up coffee for you before, and I've seen how much sugar he puts in your cup. I don't see why you bother with the coffee."

"Why do you bother at all? There's absolutely nothing in that cup when you get it."

"James says the same thing. In fact, he calls it a cup of nothing."

The barista handed them their coffees, and they took a table by the window. No one spoke for the first few minutes.

"How long have you known James?" Danielle asked. She figured she'd get it out of the way. Would it make a difference to her if their relationship was long-term, or an instant attraction they acted on in haste? Allie and James both said it wasn't what she thought, but that's what a guilty person would say.

"All my life really. He was there from the beginning."

Danielle sipped her coffee. "That's what it was like for my parents. They knew each other since birth. It was as if they were born for each other." The weight in her chest made it hard to breathe. She looked down at the words written on her hand. *Don't be an idiot. Work is for work.*

"James and I were not born to be together." She touched her chin and appeared to choose her words carefully. "We have a long history, but it's not sexual. I'd hate to lose you over a misunderstanding. You're an asset to Luxe."

"I don't really want to leave, but I can't work in a place where I'm reminded of what I lost each day."

Allie reached over and touched her graffitied skin. "You're not an idiot, and work will get better."

"I'm awful at choosing good men, but I'm good at my job. Only one of those makes me an idiot."

"I hear Chris is your ex-husband. You've been working at the resort with him for years."

A bitter laugh broke free. "Chris wasn't much of a loss."

"Let James explain. If after he discloses his secrets, and you still want to quit, I'll reluctantly accept your resignation."

"James has secrets? Can it get any worse? First, I think he's cheating, which you say is not the case. Now there are secrets. That's worse. Secrets are the cousin of lies, and I don't do lies."

Allie motioned to button her lip. "You have to talk to James. Now tell me about your interviewees."

For the next thirty minutes, everything seemed normal. If the constant ache in her heart wasn't there, she could pretend it was nearing noon again, and she'd be having lunch with James, but that wasn't the case. It was nearing three, and she was on her way to confront him. What were his secrets?

Chapter 20

JAMES

With a cup of coffee in his hand, James stepped out of the lounge just as Dani and Allie exited the elevator. He followed them into the area where their offices were. Dani entered hers and closed the door.

Maybe it wasn't such a bad idea to put glass as her office wall. At least he could see her, even if she was scowling at him.

"I can't believe it," his sister squealed from the office across from Dani's. "Why didn't you tell me the furniture came? Now I can move out of that room."

He turned and walked inside. "I was going to tell you but ..." He turned to look at Dani, who was on the phone. "Everything went to shit."

"Danielle and I talked. She'll be okay."

"What did you tell her?" Panic made his voice pitch like a pubescent teen. "You didn't tell her everything, did you?"

"No, I told her to talk to you about your secrets."

"Geez, Allie, why would you say it was a secret? Now she'll think I've been lying to her."

She moved around the room like it was hers. "You have been."

He shook his head so hard it made him dizzy. "Not true. I may have omitted some facts, but I never lied to her."

"Men and your details."

"You're impossible." He took her hand and led her out of the office. "That's my office." He marched her down the hallway and guided her into the room next door. "This is yours. Now, what did you tell her?"

"That you and I have a non-sexual history." She sat in her chair and kicked off her heels. "I'm not sure she's convinced, but at least she's now focusing on the secrets."

"I'll talk to her." He spun around and walked out.

"Give her time," Allie called after him.

"I can't," he mumbled. "I'm desperate."

When he passed Dani's office, she was still on the phone.

She saw him looking in her window and turned around so he couldn't see her face. Not one to give up easily, he paced the hallway for several minutes, waiting for her to hang up. Back and forth, he walked, trying to figure out what to say.

Did he come out of the gate with, "I'm falling in love with you," or did he start with, "I'm not who you think I am?" He let out a growl that would send most people running. "I'll figure it out when I get there."

He approached her door and knocked. He could hear her voice rise and fall with each sentence. She laughed, but it wasn't the kind of laugh that came from joy. This was a cackle that came from disbelief or hysteria.

Not willing to wait another moment to explain himself, he opened the door and peeked inside.

"Dani," he began.

She turned around and held up a single finger to stop him.

"Trish, I have to go." She ended the call and stared. "I have nothing to say to you right now."

He moved inside and shut the door. He considered rounding the desk and falling to his knees to beg for forgiveness, but he reminded himself there was nothing to forgive.

"Good, because I've got plenty to say to you." He took a seat in the chair in front of her desk. "Allie isn't my lover." A shudder ran through him at the thought. "She's my sister."

Silence ate up several long seconds while she appeared to digest his words. When her eyes grew as big as baseballs, he knew she'd fully grasped the meaning of what he'd said.

"Oh. My. God. If she's your sister, then that means—"

"I'm not her lover," he blurted.

Her head shook back and forth. "No ... you're my boss." She pushed back from the desk and jumped to her feet. "I thought you two were a thing, but this ... this is worse. You lied to me."

"I never lied to you." He stood, but she backed away as if he were a threat.

All he wanted to do was comfort her—pull her into his arms and hold her. Tell her everything would be all right, but would it? He caused her pain. Pain he saw in her eyes, and the way her shoulders slumped as if the weight he'd placed on them was too heavy to bear.

She gasped. "People will think I got this position because I slept with you."

"No one will say anything." No one better say anything. He wouldn't tolerate vicious rumors about Dani.

"Holy hell, did I get this job because we had sex?"

It wasn't the right time to laugh, but he did. "Think about it, Dani."

She stared at him in disbelief. "You think this is funny?"

"No, I don't. But I find it laughable that you believe you got the job because we slept together. Do the math. You had it before we shared our first kiss."

She fisted her hips. "Why did I get this job?"

"You want the truth?"

"I deserve the truth." She sneered. "Are you capable of telling it?" Her words bit painfully at him.

"You weren't my first choice. Not because you're not qualified, but because I thought Flynn was better suited. He has experience managing larger teams. I got outvoted by my sister and Julian, who thought taking Flynn out of the kitchen was a mistake."

Her hand came to her chest. "Ouch."

"Yes, the truth sometimes hurts, but you're doing an amazing job. I was wrong. You are the right person for the position."

"How big of you to admit your error in judgment. Since we're on a roll here, care to continue?" She backed up and leaned against the wall. "I told you I didn't date people I worked with, and you said we didn't work together."

"We don't work together. I run the construction end of the company."

"It's all in the details, right? Too bad you didn't give them to me." She opened her bottom drawer and took out her purse, then plunked it on the desktop. "I don't work with you. I work under you. Hell, I've been under you, and you don't think that's a problem?"

"Not for me," he said with a shrug.

She fisted her hips and stomped her heel onto the marble floor she loved. "It's a big deal for me."

He didn't see why it should be a big problem for her. They'd been discreet. Not many people knew about their relationship. Even if everyone did, who cared? They were adults and could separate their personal and professional lives.

"Before we made love, I asked you if it would matter if I was something else, and you said no."

"I didn't expect you to be my boss." Her hand came up to her mouth. "Oh my God, you used me to spy on everyone. I told you things about people ... about myself I wouldn't have shared if I knew."

He cocked his head to the side. "What you're telling me now is you would have withheld information if it was best for you?"

"That's not what I'm saying, and you know it."

"That's exactly what you're saying, but you won't admit it, or ... it only works when it benefits you."

"You're worse than Chris. At least I knew him."

The comparison to her ex sliced through him like a knife. "I'm nothing like Chris."

"You're right." She threw a few things from her desk into her purse and hiked it over her shoulder. "Congratulations, you're not a cheater, just a liar." She marched past him.

Chapter 21

DANIELLE

Her gift to the world was poor judgment. As the elevator descended, her heart fell with it. How was she supposed to manage a resort when she couldn't control her life?

When she exited, her spirits were low. Her anxiety was high. Hurt and betrayal swirled inside her like a cyclone.

"Duped again."

"You okay, Danielle?"

Not paying attention was becoming a habit of hers. She turned to the voice and found Paul walking toward her. It surprised her to see him anywhere beyond the security surveillance room.

"Yes." She hated the lie, but she had no intention of telling him the truth. She was anything but okay. "I'm not feeling up to par today. I'll be gone the rest of the afternoon."

He laid a meaty hand on her shoulder. "You look pale."

She tried to make a joke and pointed to the fluorescent lights that hung above. "It's all in the lighting." She wrestled a smile to her face. "Good to see you walking around. Looks like you're getting closer to asking that cutie in the gift shop out for that date."

His cheeks turned pink. "A man can dream."

She pressed the unlock button on her key fob and climbed inside her SUV. "Yes, dreaming is good." She closed the door and waved to him as she pulled out of the garage.

"Dreaming is good. It's the waking part that's a bitch."

When she arrived at home, she found a case of body chocolate on her porch and burst into tears. She lugged it inside and left it on the kitchen counter. What was she supposed to do with a case of chocolate that would remind her of him?

She changed into sweatpants and a T-shirt and sent Trish an SOS, which meant she needed wine and a shoulder to cry on.

In her kitchen sat the ingredients to the cake she'd been making with no success for weeks. Her failures were probably because she didn't pay attention to the details.

She opened the worn cover and turned to the recipe for Forever Fudge Cake. She hadn't taken the time to read the story written above the ingredient list. She'd skipped through it all to get to the good stuff—the cake. Maybe that was her problem. Had she been racing forward and missed everything in between?

She made herself a cup of coffee and took a seat at the kitchen island. She didn't want to think about forever, but cake sounded good.

She started at the beginning.

Dear Baker,

There's nothing more satisfying than a dark chocolate fudge cake. It's like a delicious hug. Why Forever Fudge Cake, you might ask? Forever is a funny concept because it sounds like it could be a long time, but forever is the moment you're in right now. You have this second. The next isn't guaranteed.

The first time I prepared this cake, I cried into the batter because my boyfriend broke my heart. It was nineteen forty-two, and he left me to join the war effort.

I was so angry at him. I was in love, and he was leaving. The odds weren't great that he'd return.

The next time I made this cake was the day he came back. He showed up on my doorstep with a smile and a ring. I could have called this Forgiveness Fudge Cake because it took about ten seconds for me to forgive him for leaving. Forgiveness comes from the heart, and my Sam said I had a big one.

My heart belonged to Sam for 55 years when he left me again. He didn't have a choice, and he wasn't coming back, but I know he'll be waiting for me and a slice of this cake.

As you mix the ingredients, think about the minutes in your life. How do you want to spend them? Unlike Sam, you have a choice about how your forever goes.

Adelaide Phelps

"Some choice," she huffed.

Danielle gathered the ingredients and measured them out perfectly. She even took into account the altitude. She wasn't looking for forever. That dream had died when she found out she'd been sleeping with the man who signed her paychecks.

Nope, all she wanted was a chocolate cake and a bottle of wine.

She mixed everything together, including the monkey butt bar of chocolate, and poured it into pans before she slid them onto the center rack of the preheated oven. When she turned around, her doorbell rang.

She rushed forward, hoping it was Trish but scared it was James. What would she say to him if he stood on her doorstep begging for forgiveness?

She peeked through the peephole and was both relieved and shattered when she saw Trish.

"You came."

"I'll always come. You're my best friend. I would have walked in, but my hands were full." She held up a bottle of wine and a gallon of birthday cake ice cream. "I brought emotional Band-Aids. Now, tell me what happened after we spoke."

Danielle led her into the kitchen, where she grabbed two glasses and two spoons. If she thought Trish would share nicely, they could have drunk straight from the bottle, but she knew Trish. With wine, she had a two for her and one for everyone else rule.

"It got worse."

"Worse than him cheating on you?"

Danielle wasn't sure where to start, and since the story was bitter and painful, she grabbed a spoon, opened the ice cream and took a big bite while Trish poured the wine.

"So much worse," she said with a full mouth. She swallowed and immediately regretted that move. Brain freeze had her squinting, holding her breath, and counting the seconds until the discomfort went away.

Trish took a seat beside her and rolled her wineglass between her palms. "How's that possible?"

"He didn't cheat on me."

Trish looked at her like she was speaking in tongues. "I don't get it. That's great. You should be happy."

"Allie isn't his lover, but his sister. She wouldn't tell me that because he needed to come clean on his own."

It took Trish a few seconds to put the pieces together, and when she did, she picked up her glass and emptied it in one go.

"No fu ... lipping way."

Danielle told her everything she could remember. It was all a blur at this point. The only real words she could say verbatim were, "Allie isn't my lover. She's my sister." And at the end of her telling, Trish took a spoon and scooped up a bite of ice cream. Danielle had already worked herself through a third of the container.

"Let me get this straight. He's handsome and rich and good in bed?"

"That's all irrelevant, but yes, he'd be a four-fecta if he were honest." The ice cream sat heavy in her gut and threatened to come back up. She pushed it toward Trish, who happily tucked it in her arm and dug in. "I tried to quit, but Allie wouldn't accept my resignation. How am I supposed to work there?" She pointed to the stack of bills sitting on the edge of the counter. "How can I quit?"

"You act like he used you. He didn't. He was into you."

Danielle groaned. "Don't remind me."

"I mean, he liked you and probably still does." Trish set the ice cream bucket down and reached for the pile of bills. "A man like him could take care of these with one check."

"I don't need a man to rescue me. All I want is a man to love me and loving me means he has to be honest."

"Not true." Trish took the wine bottle and poured herself another splash but didn't fill her glass. "Love means doing what you feel is right. What you know is right. Have you stopped to consider his motives? Maybe he was looking for someone to love him for who he is and not what he has. Has it ever occurred to you that having his kind of money could be a curse and not the blessing everyone thinks it is?"

Her heart lurched. She realized Trish was talking from her own experience. She always questioned people's motives, and rightly so, because many men had professed their love to her. Only they weren't interested in her affections, just her net worth.

In some way, that's how it had been with Chris. She made more money than him. She had a better credit score. He didn't marry her because he was in love with her. He married her because she was a way to extend his credit so he could live outside his budget.

"Don't decide about your job or James without considering everything. Those decisions are forever. You've got time to make the right choice."

Her words were eerily similar to Adelaide Phelps and her Forever Fudge Cake story.

"You're right. I'll take some time to think it through."

"All of it. Including James. He's a good man." She tapped her heart with her fist. "I feel it here." Trish filled Danielle's glass. "I'd love to stay, but I have a date with Rob and body paints." She kissed Danielle on the cheek and lifted her nose in the air. "The cake smells amazing. It'll go great with that other half-gallon of ice cream or a jar of chocolate."

"Don't remind me. You can take it off my hands."

Trish shook her head. "I'll let you know when I run out."

Danielle walked her to the door and stood there until Trish drove away.

Was it possible to be right and wrong about a man? Deep inside, she knew he was good too, but could she forgive him?

She went back into the kitchen. While she waited for the timer to ding, she read Adelaide Phelps's message about forever again. It played through her mind on repeat. *Think about the minutes in your life. How do you want to spend them? You have a choice about how your forever goes.*

When the cake cooled, she frosted it and took a bite. It was moist. The frosting was creamy. The cake was perfect, and she had no one to share it with.

Chapter 22

JAMES

James lugged box after box to Allie's and Julian's offices. He volunteered to do anything that might get him closer to Dani, but she'd found every reason to avoid him.

She showed up for work each morning but made training her replacement for the Guest Services Department a priority. He couldn't fault her. They hired her to make sure the resort ran efficiently, and the guests were happy, but he wasn't happy. Outside of a cursory glance here and there, she acted as if he didn't exist.

"Two weeks, Allie. Two damn weeks and she hasn't spoken to me." He hoisted the last of her boxes onto her desk.

Julian sat in the armchair decorating the corner. "Why would you need one woman when you can have all the women? You're thinking with the wrong head, man."

A book whizzed by James and hit Julian in the shoulder. His sister always had perfect aim. "You can be such a jerk. That's why you sleep alone."

Julian leaned back and swiped right and left on his phone. "You shouldn't throw rocks at glass houses, sweetheart."

"I'm not." She gave him a smile that would bring most men to their knees, but not Julian because Allie was as close to a sibling as he could get. "I'm throwing a book at your meathead. Swiping right doesn't make it right. I sleep alone because I have exacting standards for men." She opened the box and pulled out the pictures of their family. She always decorated her office to feel like home. She spent more time there than she did anywhere else. Julian could have a point. Were her standards too high?

"You set the bar up there next to Christ," Julian said. "Good luck with that."

Allie picked up another book and pulled back like she would throw it, but instead, she placed it on the empty bookshelf. "Maybe, if you had some standards, your life would be different."

Julian rolled his eyes. "I've got standards. They have to be breathing and willing."

"The pool of candidates must be impressive." She started placing the pictures. She had several of James and her growing up. They lived a privileged existence with winter ski trips in the Alps and summer vacations in Bora Bora. It was how they went into the resort business. Every place they visited, they'd sit down and tell each other what they'd do differently. Julian came on board because while he was an arrogant asshole, he was an amazing bean counter. Not once had they been caught unaware or unprepared with the purchase of a property. They always knew how much money and time it would take to recoup their investment. Luxe at Timberline was their riskiest purchase to date.

Putting his focus on the conversation, he listened as Allie and Julian lobbed insults back and forth. He waved his hand into the air. "Hello, we were talking about me."

"Right, and I offered sage advice. Find another woman."

That was the most ridiculous advice ever. "There's no one like her. She's amazing. She's strong but vulnerable. Intelligent and humble. She's—"

"Standing right behind you." Allie put her hand over her mouth, but he could still hear her laugh.

Julian rolled to his feet. "I don't do conflict. I'll be in my office if you need me." He approached Dani. "Good to see you, Danielle. You're doing an excellent job."

"Thank you." She looked at Allie. "Are you ready?"

"Ready for what?" James moved toward her, but she gave him a raised palm and a shake of her head.

"Not yet."

He was happy to see her give him a whole hand when it could be just a middle finger.

"Let me get my purse. It's in the conference room. Stay here, I'll be back." While Allie searched for her purse, Dani stepped toward the bookshelf and held up a framed photo. It was one of his favorites, taken in Aspen at Snowmass after Allie broke her leg hotdogging down a black diamond run. They were inseparable for six weeks. He'd carried her everywhere because he felt responsible.

He moved quietly behind Dani. "I helped break her leg." He was close enough to smell her perfume and notice her breath catch when his words floated across her skin.

"Proud moment?" She put the picture down but didn't move.

"I felt about as proud as I do right now, which isn't at all. I'm sorry, Dani. I'm so damn sorry."

Allie rushed around the corner. "Got it." She held up her bag. "I'm ready now."

"Where are you guys going?" He'd never been jealous of his sister until that moment. She was exactly where he wanted to be—on Dani's good side.

"I don't know," Allie said. "Dinner? Movie? Dancing?" Her eyes lit up. "There's that new place in Aspen called Heartbeat."

"That's a pickup joint," he said.

Dani walked past him. "So, you've been there?"

"No." He thought better of the lie. "I mean yes, but it was with Julian, and before you and I ..." The turn of events completely flustered him. He'd finally gotten in the same room with Dani. She'd said more than a curt hello, and now she was going clubbing with his sister?

"Don't wait up for me." Allie kissed him on the cheek as she passed.

They were going to Heartbeat, and he was certain his had stopped. He left the offices and went home to change. He wasn't ready to give up on Dani. She refused to look at him, but he'd make sure she couldn't ignore him.

An hour later, he sat at the bar, sipping a club soda and watching the door. They had obviously taken a detour, or maybe they weren't coming. That thought brought a sigh of relief until Allie appeared. She marched in, talking to herself. The bouncer looked at her like she was crazy. When she realized she was alone, she stomped out the door and dragged Dani in.

The ceasing of his heartbeat minutes before started to blip and beat. She didn't want to be there, and that made him happy.

He ordered Dani a glass of red wine and his sister a vodka gimlet. When they approached the bar, the drinks were ready.

"What are you doing here?" Allie asked.

"Watching out for my girls." He handed them their glasses. "Here's to an enjoyable evening."

"You weren't invited," Dani said.

He looked around. "Is this a private party?"

"You know what I mean." She sipped her wine and glanced at Allie for help.

He knew his sister, and she knew him. It was why she dropped the name of the bar and pulled Dani inside. There was no way he wouldn't be sitting there waiting.

"There's Buffy Buffington." His sister squealed and pointed to a person across the room. She picked up her gimlet and disappeared into the crowd.

Dani looked around for a way to escape.

"Take my seat. Your feet must be killing you."

She reluctantly traded places with him and couldn't help the sigh when she sat down. "Thank you." She lifted a few inches and searched the crowd. "There isn't a Buffy Buffington is there?"

He shook his head. "Not that I know of. If there was, I feel sorry for the woman."

"Your sister's as manipulative as you are. Must run in the genes."

He got bumped from behind, forcing him to move closer. Music started, and it drowned their voices out. He bent over so she could hear him. "She loves me. This wasn't my plan. I can't say if it was hers. But I want to be where you are, and so here I am." He held out a hand. "I know your feet hurt, and you're angry at me but dance with me. Just one dance. Please?"

She stared at his hand like he hadn't washed it in days. After what seemed like forever, she put her palm in his and allowed him to lead her to the dance floor. The song playing wasn't slow by any means, but he pulled her into his arms and swayed to the music. Just feeling the warmth of her body tucked next to him was more than he could hope for.

"Is your name really James?" She leaned back and looked into his eyes.

He closed his and thanked the gods. She was still there, in his arms, and asking questions.

"Yes. My birth name is Alistair James Parks, JR. I go by James. You could have looked me up. I'm sure there are pictures of me on the internet."

"I looked you up on the website for Luxe when your company took over the resort. There weren't any photos."

He nodded. "We were updating the site to include the new location. Since our photos were a decade old, we were waiting for when we hired a photographer to shoot the new pictures of the hotel." His hand moved gently up and down her back.

"Very convenient."

He let out a sigh. She was not going to forgive him easily. "Not really. I didn't hide my identity from you. I go by James. We didn't use only first names in the resort so I could get you into bed.

Normally, all I have to do is say my last name, and that works just fine."

He hadn't meant to cause her pain, but his words seemed to do just that. Then again, maybe he had said them to hurt her like she was hurting him. He wasn't sure at this point. All he knew was that not being with her was torture.

"Look," he stood back and took her in as the crowd moved around them. "Nothing I did was meant to mislead you. I'm in charge of the construction. I go in as undercover boss all the time. It puts people at ease."

"You're the friendly plant to get people to trust you and talk to you and sleep with you?"

He shook his head and led her back to the bar where his seat was still open. "No, I'm the CEO, but I rarely use that moniker. I prefer hands-on. I enjoy mingling with the staff."

She took the seat and finished her wine, then set her empty glass on the bar. "Is that what we were doing. Were we mingling?"

He wanted to take hold of her shoulders and shake some sense into her. Pull her into his arms again, but this time kiss her until she knew exactly who he was. He was the same man she'd made love to weeks ago.

"Dani, I care about you. What we had together was ..."

"Wasn't authentic."

Rob's statement came back to mind. *Authenticity is hard to find these days.*

"You're right. I made a mistake. You might not have known my birth name or my actual title in the company, but you know me." He grabbed her hand and placed it over his heart. "I'm the same man who made love to you for hours on end because there was nothing in the world more important than pleasing you. Damn it, Dani, just give me a chance to prove I'm trustworthy."

She pulled her hand away and slid off the bar stool. "I need to go."

"I'll drive you." He pulled two twenties from his wallet and laid them on the bar. "Please, just let me get you home. I won't press you for anything. I won't even talk the whole way to your house. All I'm asking is for you to not shut me out."

She nodded. "Let me find your sister to tell her I'm leaving."

He chuckled. "Sweetheart, she's probably already home and in her bunny slippers crocheting another lap blanket."

"You two are a tag team."

"Like I said, she loves me and I ... well, you'll figure it out." He wanted to shout he loved her, but he knew the words would send her running out the door to flag down the first ride she could find.

He placed his hand on her back and walked her to his truck.

As promised, he didn't say a word the whole way. She needed to trust him, and promises were important. Apparently, as important as transparency. If she wanted to know everything about him, he'd deliver his resume.

When he pulled up to her cottage, he parked and raced around to open her door.

"I got it from here." She turned toward him, and for a second, he thought she'd lean in and kiss him. She rocked forward then stepped back. "Thank you for the ride. I'll see you tomorrow."

"You will. I'll be there. Smiling. Waiting. Hoping." He stayed until she disappeared inside, and he heard the lock click. He turned around and skipped down her sidewalk. Things were still grim. He was a long way from cuddling up next to her warm naked body, but his chances were looking up.

EARLY THE NEXT MORNING, his phone dinged with an incoming email. His heart soared when he saw Dani's name and her request for an impromptu meeting. Had she forgiven him?

He dressed for work and raced to the office. When he arrived at the designated meeting space, his heart sank to see Julian and Allie at the table.

Was this it? Would she walk in and hand them her resignation letter?

The *tip-tap* of her heels echoed through the hallway. Dressed in a black suit and pink blouse, she entered the room looking like she could conquer the world. She handed out folders and stared him straight in the eye. "We have a problem."

Chapter 23

DANIELLE

Her chest ached after seeing James at Heartbeat. It nearly broke when she left him outside and walked into her cottage alone. She'd tossed and turned for the first two hours after she'd climbed in bed. Since she couldn't sleep, she plugged in the flash drive she brought home and went over Chris's inventory. Nothing made sense. She'd pulled last year's records for his department.

No matter how she sliced and diced the numbers, they never added up. His equipment orders didn't match the inventory, and little was removed for damage. She figured he'd been ordering supplies and selling it on the side. There was also the possibility that he'd pocketed cash payments instead of charging services to the rooms. Chris had a profitable side business. His wasn't a soft bonus but a perpetual heist. She considered ignoring the discrepancies because acknowledging them created an avalanche of problems from having to confront her ex to picking up his car payments when he could no longer afford to make them.

But knowing something and not acting on the information made her an awful general manager. In a way, she'd be no better than

James. How could she be so angry with him when she considered doing something as sneaky because it served her?

She couldn't imagine what Chris planned to do when the resort was complete, and they moved over to an all-inclusive model. It wouldn't matter because she had to do the right thing and let him go.

"Thank you for coming on such short notice. I've spent several days trying to make sense of Avis' system and fear there may be bigger problems than you considered when you bought The Pines. I'm sure Julian is aware of the discrepancies, but I thought I'd show you where the bulk of them are coming from."

She went over the profit and loss for each department, and when she got to Outdoor Recreation, she showed how he'd been giving himself generous bonuses for a long time.

Allie cleared her throat. "What are you going to do about that?"

Danielle took a seat next to James. Maybe it was because Allie and Julian sat on one side of the table or maybe because he was alone. She didn't have time to analyze her seat choice. She sat and inhaled a big breath.

"I'll fire him." She looked at James because he knew her background. Allie knew as well, but she wasn't sure if Julian was informed. "There might be a problem because I was once married to Chris, and he'll claim it's an unfair termination because it's personal. He could file a hostile work environment complaint. I wanted you to know up front because it might get ugly before it gets better."

Allie watched her for a moment and nodded. "I'll take care of it. He can complain to human resources all he wants. That's my department until I find a perfect fit."

The tension coiled inside Danielle loosened. She hadn't realized she'd been holding her breath until she exhaled, and the group stared at her.

"You know what?" James said. "I've got this."

Everyone looked at him and then at Julian to see if he had any input.

"Don't look at me," Julian said. "I'm the numbers guy, not the executioner."

James tucked the report back into the folder. "I said I'll deal with it."

Danielle turned her chair to face him. She had hoped she could have had one day where the entire universe wasn't fighting her. She didn't mind if Allie handled it because it fell in her department, but if James fired Chris, it became personal. Her ex-boyfriend firing her ex-husband wasn't right.

"I don't need you to rescue me. I'll take care of this situation on my own."

He laid his hands on the table and stared straight ahead. "I realize you don't need me at all, but I'm here, and I said I'd take care of it."

She did her best to remain calm. The released tension tightened again. Only this time, Chris and his lying and cheating weren't to blame. She couldn't come to terms with how she felt about James.

Everyone around her said to give him another chance. Her heart wanted that, but her head wasn't sure.

She faced him with a defiant lift of her chin. "Needing you isn't what this is about." She leaned in. "Can't we talk about this later?" She turned toward Julian and Allie, who watched them like a blockbuster movie.

James' jaw clenched until a muscle in his cheek twitched. "My involvement in this situation is not because I'm rescuing you but because I'm taking care of the company. A wrongful termination lawsuit could drag Luxe into the mud for years. I have the evidence, and I'll present it professionally. Our attorney can sit in if that makes everyone feel more comfortable."

Allie gave a sturdy nod. "I think that's a brilliant idea. That way, if you kick his ass, you'll have counsel there when the police pick you up."

He looked at Dani. "He deserves a good ass-kicking."

"I could name a few men that deserve at least that," she gathered her papers and laid her hands on her folder.

Allie stood, "You ready for coffee?" she asked Danielle.

"Bar hopping last night and coffee today? When did you two become such good friends?" James asked.

His sister was quick with a reply. "When she found out you and I weren't lovers."

Julian laughed like a howler monkey. "That's my cue to leave." He picked up his folder and walked out.

With the skill of an award-winning actress, Allie touched her forehead with the back of her hand. "Coffee is my apology for leaving early last night. I had something or another."

"Lying doesn't suit you," James said.

"Learning from you, big brother. I've heard that omission isn't the same as a lie. I didn't say I was leaving … sorry. Not sorry."

Danielle watched the exchange between siblings. Their words were severe, sharp, and designed to draw blood with a single slice. She had two sisters. They'd defend each other to the ends of the earth, but they'd also deliver the most painful blows. It was the way with siblings.

"Can you give me and Dani a moment?"

"Yep, but just a moment. I need a grande cup of nothing, bad." Allie walked past them, the *clickety-clack* of her heels fading down the hallway.

Danielle looked around the empty room. It was just the two of them. Was it possible to feel trapped despite a wall of windows and an open door?

He leaned toward her and cupped her cheek. "You look tired. Are you okay?"

She shook her head no, but a yes came out of her mouth. "Yes, I'm okay. I worked on the report all night."

"Are you sure it was the report that kept you up?"

Her hand came up to cover his. God how she missed him, but to give in so easily would send the wrong message. Not to him, but to herself.

She thought about Trish's last piece of advice. "Don't decide about your job or James without considering everything. Those decisions are forever. You've got time to make the right choice." What was the right choice?

"No, I had a lot of things on my mind. There's the new job and the old job. Past. Present. Future. They are all coming together at once."

He closed the gap between them and pressed his forehead to hers. "I want to be part of your future, Dani. I messed up. I'll make it up to you. If I had it to do all over again, I would trap you inside the plastic sheeting and tell you everything."

She dropped her hand. "I need some time. One thing I learned over the last few weeks is that in order to love someone else, I have to be okay with who I am first. I'm not sure where I stand with me." She pushed her chair back and stood. "I'll see you later."

"You will?"

She made a half effort to smile. "Sure, we work together."

"We do," he said. "We're a team. A good team."

He walked her to the door. Half tempted to turn around and kiss him, she forced herself forward. She wasn't the type to pull him in and push him back. Mixed messages didn't serve anyone well.

She stopped several feet from him and turned around. "You need anything?" she asked.

"Yes, but I'll wait until you're ready to give it to me."

"Let's go," Allie said, walking past her. "I need coffee like a junkie needs a fix." She threaded her arm through Danielle's and tugged her along.

All the while, Danielle looked over her shoulder at James. He leaned on the doorjamb and watched her walk away. Sadness and regret showed in the dullness of his whiskey-colored eyes.

When the elevator arrived, and they stepped inside, Allie asked, "Are you ever going to give my brother another chance?"

"I don't know. I can't decide if his omission was a minor error in judgment or a deal-breaker."

The elevator opened in the garage, and they walked up the ramp to the street. "There are no perfect men, Danielle, just the perfect man for you."

"I'm not asking for perfection. If I were, your brother is damn close. All I asked for was honesty." They crossed the street and walked inside Pikes Perk. Both lifted their noses into the air and breathed deeply.

"Who needs meditation when there's espresso?" Danielle said.

Allie laughed. "That's like saying who needs men when there are vibra ... I mean chocolate."

"That's not what you meant."

"No, but you got my meaning."

They ordered their coffees and took a seat by the window.

"So ... back to my brother. I know you care for him. It shows in your eyes."

"I do but—"

"But what?"

"I was just getting to a place where I could trust, and he ruined that."

"Don't lie to yourself. You weren't at that place of trust yet. You're still in the mode to punish all men for whatever your ex did to you. If you can't let that go, I'd rather you didn't care for my brother because he doesn't deserve punishment for another man's mistakes. Hang him from the rafters because he didn't tell you he was the CEO. He never lied to you. You simply didn't ask the right questions."

Maybe she was right. Was she being too hard on him? Punishing him for the sins of all worthless men?

"I'm scared."

"Who isn't? It's okay to be scared, just don't be a coward. It's better to love and lose then not love at all or some shit like that."

"Here you are, giving me advice, but what about you? Anyone special in your life?"

Allie choked on her coffee. "No, I haven't found a guy worth getting scared over. People like James and Julian and I have to be more careful with dating and relationships. Imagine having to wonder if someone is interested in you for the right reasons."

She'd heard that a lot lately. "There's a thing called a prenup."

"Yep, I had one drawn up once."

"You were engaged?"

She nodded. "The second I said that word was the second he left. I guess I could thank the stars that it ended before it really began. Prenup is the stage right before marriage, divorce, and alimony." She laughed. "It's a vicious cycle."

Allie downed her coffee and stood. "Ready to get back to work? I believe you have to recruit some hunky outdoorsman for the position being vacated this week."

"Maybe a cute outdoorswoman would be better."

Allie shook her head. "Can't drink the hater aide. Not all men are bad. Find the best person for the job. Man or woman is great, and if it's a goat, I'm fine with that too."

Chapter 24

JAMES

The week had been a long one. He waited in the conference room for Chris to show up. He was late. He didn't want to burden Dani with another position to fill, but she was right. He was siphoning money at a three to one ratio with the lion's share going into his pocket.

It only took their investigator a day to find the site where the idiot sold his stolen goods. It took three more days for James to lay it all out in a report basic enough for Chris to understand.

The idiot walked into the conference room in board shorts and Vans and raised his hands like a rock star. "I'm here."

James wasn't in the mood for games. He despised this man for many reasons. The biggest being how he'd treated Dani.

He clenched and unclenched his fists. It would have been so easy to bolt from his seat and destroy the asshole, but this was business.

He pointed to the empty chair to his left. "Have a seat."

"Is this about a job?" He looked between the lawyer and James. "Didn't expect you to be here."

James ignored the question for now. He introduced the man on his right. "Chris Putnam, this is Michael Stratton, our legal representative from Stratton, Walton, and Winslow." He loved that they were big enough clients to get the man whose name was listed first in the firm.

Chris eyed the man suspiciously. "I take it I'm not here for a promotion."

James sat there for a few minutes. "You're perceptive this afternoon. You must have eaten your Wheaties and had your multivitamin. Flintstones, right?"

Michael cleared his throat. It was a warning for James to keep it professional. He passed a folder to Chris and asked him to turn to page one.

"What's this?"

This was the part James would enjoy immensely. "This is where I tell you, you're fired."

"You can't fire me. You're just a construction guy."

James smiled. "Forgive me. I should have introduced myself." He offered him a handshake. "I'm Alistair James Parks, and I own Luxe with my partners Allie and Julian. You can call me James."

It took Chris a minute to process what he heard. "You're my boss?"

"Since you're obviously low on the evolutionary chain, I'll explain. Your boss is Danielle. Technically, I fall above that position."

"Does Danielle know you're firing me?" He looked down at the paper where a highlighted mid-five figure number glowed like the sun.

"She's aware of the issue, but since you have a history, the management thought it best to deal with the problem." He turned to Michael. "I think this is a good time for you to take over."

Michael leaned forward and pointed to the highlighted total. "This is the amount you've stolen this year alone."

"Is that what she's saying?" His eyes grew big, and his face grew red. "You know she's my ex-wife and bitter about the divorce."

James pulled his hands from the table and pushed them under his thighs for restraint. "We're aware of the past relationship. Danielle was forthcoming with the information when she pointed out the discrepancies."

"I want a recount."

James and Michael laughed.

"This isn't an election or a hanging chad issue," Michael said. "The numbers don't lie. The amount circled is for this year alone."

"She's lying," Chris yelled. "That bitch is punishing me because she's lacking."

James was about to fly out of his seat when Michael set his hand on his shoulder. It was a reminder to keep this professional.

"We have done an in-depth investigation." He pulled a piece of paper that included a picture of Chris's shop and the inventory he had listed. Items identical to the missing inventory. "As we see it, you have one option. You can leave quietly, and there won't be a problem."

"Or," he said with sly smile. "I can sue the hell out of you for wrongful termination. Don't forget, Dani is a spurned woman."

James' insides were at the boiling point. He couldn't say a word for fear he'd jump across the table and choke the bastard to death.

Michael piped in. "You can fight this." He circled the amount over and over again. "I'd be happy to go back and audit all the years you've worked here."

They waited and watched for his reaction. When there wasn't one, Michael continued. "Your current theft is already past the grand larceny limit." He brushed off the left lapel of his jacket. "Right now, it's a class four felony and up to six years in prison, but I'm certain after further investigation we could get that to a class three and twelve years."

"This is bullshit."

"This is your reality. Either you accept the agreement, or you go to prison. It's not that difficult of a choice to make."

Chris stood. "What about a severance package?"

"What about no jail time. That's the deal." Michael pulled his cell phone from his pocket. "Take it or leave it. If you decide to leave it, I'll call the police, and you can negotiate with them."

Chris raised his hands in mock surrender. "Fine. I'm out."

"Not yet," Michael said. "You need to sign this form stating that you agree to the terms of this mediation and are leaving after considering your options."

"This is coercion."

"No, this is kindness," James said. "If it were up to me, you'd already be in prison."

Chris eyed them both. "So, if I sign that paper, you won't press charges, and I won't go to jail?"

"Only the prison you put yourself in because of your stupidity," James added.

Michael gave him a look that said to shut up, but he needed something to make him feel better. This man had stolen from the company, from Dani, and, in a way, from him. If he hadn't betrayed her trust, she might have some left to give.

Chris signed the paper, and James called Paul to escort him from the property.

When Michael left, James returned to his office. The one right across the hall from Dani's.

Allie walked in. "Did it go well?"

"Yes, he's not our problem anymore." He ran his hands through his hair. "How could someone so intelligent and lovely end up with a loser like that?" Despite his frustration he smiled. "I enjoyed firing him. It was the one thing I could do for her." He glanced across the hall to her office. The cup of coffee he put on her desk at lunch still sat there. "Have you seen her?"

"She's training her replacement—a woman named Harper Stevenson. She should be back in a few minutes." She looked at her watch. "I'm surprised you're still here. It's quitting time."

"I'm not a quitter. I'm staging a sit-in until she returns."

"Should I order you dinner? Breakfast for tomorrow? You need a pillow and one of my crocheted blankets?"

He crumpled a blank piece of paper from his desk and threw it at her. "Go home and leave me to my misery."

He sat there, staring straight ahead, waiting for Dani to return. He'd been like a cat leaving his owner a mouse as a gift each morning. Only his gift came in a twelve-ounce cup.

Every day that week, he'd put a cup of coffee on her desk. The first day, he left one packet of sugar, hoping she'd find him to tell him he got it wrong. Each day since, he'd been upping his game. Five packets. Ten. A box of sugar cubes. He stared across the hallway, looking at the untouched coffee and the five-pound bag of sugar he'd left today.

Heels *tip-tapped* on the tile floor. They weren't Allie because she walked so firmly and fast that her heels sound like rapid fire from a weapon. Danielle's walk was slow and purposeful.

She entered her office and laughed. He hadn't heard that sound in weeks, and it made his heart race. Made him feel better than the time they opened their first resort.

She pivoted and crossed the hallway in short quick strides. "What are you trying to do, give me diabetes?"

He stood and walked to her. "No, I was hoping to sweeten your disposition toward me." He reached for her but stopped because he didn't want to send her running. "I miss you so much. I miss us. Please, Dani, give me a chance."

She closed the distance between them and rested her head on his chest. "I miss us too."

With his arms folded around her, they stood there for a long moment.

"I'm sorry, James."

He stepped back so he could see her eyes. "You're sorry? I'm the one who ruined everything. I told you trust was the most important thing, and I broke your trust in me."

"I should have known you didn't do it to hurt me." Her hand settled over his heart. "It's not in you to hurt. All we can do is our best and hope we get it right. If we don't the first time, we try again."

"I hid the biggest part of who I am. I hid my wealth, my power, and my position."

She laughed. "Sweetheart, that's not the biggest part of you. Do you need a refresher?" She ran her hand down his chest, below his belt to cup his growing length.

"Does this mean we get to start over again?"

She stepped away and pointed to his desk. "Yes, but I want to renegotiate my employment contract. I'm not dating my boss."

He adjusted himself and took a seat.

He took a sheet of paper from the drawer and picked up the pen from the desk.

"Name your terms."

She pulled out the chair in front of his desk and sat like she was the interviewer and he the interviewee. There was no negotiating. He'd do anything she wanted, including leaving his position as CEO if it meant getting her back.

"I'll fall under Julian for performance reviews because neither you nor Allie can be objective. It's important I get judged for my work performance and not by my familiarity with the owners."

"Done." He jotted it down. "Next."

"I'd like you to include me in all executive meetings, so I'm not caught unaware. I think Avis knew what was going on, but she didn't have the information or the desire to stop it."

His pen moved across the paper. "Done. Anything else?"

"The rest is personal."

"I'm all ears."

"Everything will be different. I'm figuring out who I am and what I am." She leaned forward. "I'm a work in progress, but I've finally figured out what you are."

His brows lifted. "What am I?"

Her mouth tipped into a lazy, sexy smile. "Everything."

Chapter 25

DANIELLE

"Why am I so nervous?"

Trish tugged Danielle's shirt down to show more cleavage. "Because Mr. Sexy's hammer might nail you tonight."

"Maybe you're right, but I've slept with the man, and I know it will be wonderful." That part of their relationship needed no renegotiating or addendum. "I think it's because it's our first real date."

"Bullship, you went to lunch and dinner." She loved the way Trish had created her own curse words. Bullship, son of a monkey, and shitake mushroom were regulars in her vernacular. Recently, fudge nuggets hit the list.

"Okay," Danielle blurted. "I don't have an excuse, but I'm nervous because this feels like ..."

"Forever?"

"Yes." She checked herself in the mirror and made sure she didn't have flour or frosting on her face. A fancy restaurant was the plan, but now that she had him back, she didn't want to share him with anyone.

The doorbell rang, and her heart jumped into her throat.

Trish picked up her purse and gave her a kiss on the cheek. "I'll go out the back door. Go get your man."

Danielle's heart clanged like a church bell inside her chest. She raced to the door and flung it open to find James standing there with flowers.

"You ready?" he asked.

She stepped aside. "Change of plans. I ordered Chinese takeout, and I made dessert."

She led him into the kitchen, where they filled their plates with cashew chicken and shanghai beef before they stepped onto her backyard patio.

"Beautiful," he said when he took his seat next to her.

She'd decked the table out with candles and heart confetti.

"It's probably silly, but this feels like a real date."

"Does that mean I get to kiss you before I leave?"

Yesterday they made amends in his office and agreed to take things slowly. It had only been one day, but she was finished moving at a snail's pace. She didn't want bits and pieces of him. She wanted all of him. According to Adelaide Phelps, forever was the minute they had right now.

"You're leaving me?"

"Not a chance, Dani. Yesterday you stated your demands. Last night I thought about a few of my own."

She lifted from her chair. "Should I write them down?"

He took a bite of his food and chewed slowly. The man was as exasperating as he was exhilarating. "No, these are more about me than you. Promises I'll make and keep."

"I'm listening."

"I will always be honest, and I want that from you too. The truth shouldn't separate us but bring us together."

"Agreed, anything else?"

He chuckled. "I want to spend more time with you than without you."

"You want a lot, Mr. Parks."

"Oh Dani, I want it all, but if I have to settle for less just to be with you, then so be it."

"You know what I've learned?" She smiled. "Never settle for less when you can demand more."

"Agreed." He poured them a glass of wine from the bottle airing on the table.

He scanned the label and nearly dropped the bottle. "Wow, you bought the Pride Reserve. Can you afford this?" He looked around her backyard. "Are we going to dine and dash?" He lifted a foot covered with a leather loafer. "Not running shoes, but I'll keep up."

She took the bottle from him and filled their glasses to the top.

"You know James, I'm not rich, but I do okay. You don't have to worry about my bank account." She used the same wording he had on their first dinner together. Her raise afforded her many things. She wasn't at risk of foreclosure, and occasionally, she could afford a nice bottle of wine.

They enjoyed a leisurely dinner in the backyard, and when the sun set and the bottle was empty, they gathered their plates and went inside.

"How about dessert?" She pointed to a chocolate cake on the counter.

"Looks great. Where did you buy it?"

"I made it." She took two small plates from the cupboard and set them next to the cake. The knife cut through the chocolate like a hot blade moved through butter.

With two perfectly sliced pieces, she joined him at the stools by the island.

He stared at the plate but didn't pick up his fork.

"Are you going to eat it?" she asked.

He rubbed the scruff on his chin. "Are you sure you're not pretending to let me back into your life, so there's no suspicion when you poison me?"

"I hadn't considered killing you until this very second, now take a bite."

He stabbed a forkful and pulled it to his mouth, but before he could eat it, she leaned in and stole it.

She sat back and moaned and groaned. She had to admit it was amazing. Almost as good as sex—almost. "So good." She swallowed and sat up straight. "I took a bite, and I'm still here, so it must be okay."

"By the sounds you made, it has to be better than okay." He stared at the plate like it would snap at him.

"What are you waiting for?" She prodded.

"Nothing. It's just that cake isn't your superpower."

She grabbed the kitchen towel from the counter and swatted him with it. "I figured something out. The things that are most important are the hardest to perfect. Like this cake ... my previous attempts were failures, but I didn't give up. I sacrificed a lot of eggs to get it to this level of edibility." She scooped a forkful and lifted it to his mouth. "Open up, you'll love it."

He opened his mouth and took the bite. His eyes grew wide. "It is perfect." He shook his head. "But I don't love it."

"You don't?" She sounded crestfallen.

He leaned and whispered against her mouth. "No, I love you."

His lips hovered over hers until she closed the millimeters of space between them and opened her mouth to let him in. With a single sweep, she tasted his love. Arms embracing. Bodies reaching. Tongues tangling. The kiss was both everything and not enough. When they separated for a breath, he pulled her onto his lap and thumbed her chin so she couldn't look anywhere but in his eyes. Eyes that were no longer dulled by pain but brightened by passion.

"Thank you for not giving up on me," he whispered against her lips.

"Thanks for being patient." All patience had left her. She'd wasted so many minutes of her forever dwelling on the past.

"I wouldn't call me patient, but maybe persistent. You on the other hand are stubborn."

She squirmed in his lap. Every cell of her body had come to life. "Me? Stubborn?"

"And smart, and sexy as hell." He scooped up a fingerful of frosting and wiped it over her lips. "Brings back memories."

With a flick of her tongue, she tasted the fudge. "I've got a case minus two jars."

His head snapped back. "You used two jars? With who?"

She lifted her shoulders with a shrug. "Depression and desperation work hand in hand. When I ran out of ice cream, I broke into the chocolate."

He laughed so hard, his body rocked, and he nearly knocked her off his lap.

"Don't laugh at me," she said. "I've come across some great combinations. A spoonful of peanut butter and a spoonful of chocolate." She kissed her fingers and raised them in the air. "Amazing."

"Not original. That's already been done."

"Yes, but it becomes magical when you add a squeeze of strawberry jam."

He kissed her nose. "You're crazy."

"Probably, but you love me, and there are no take-backs."

"I do love you, and I'm keeping you."

She giggled. "I've never been a kept woman."

She slid from his lap to her stool.

"How does it feel to be mine?"

"It feels like I'm fully alive."

He leaned forward and made love to her mouth in the same way she knew he'd love her body. Slowly. Passionately. Thoroughly.

When they separated for a breath, he said, "I've got a question." He turned to look at the plate of cake. "Why always chocolate?"

"It's special. It's called Forever Fudge Cake."

He nodded. "I like that." He leaned in, so they were eye-to-eye. "I've got another question."

"You're just full of them tonight."

"Shall we start our forever from the beginning where I introduce myself and tell you my name is Alistair James Parks, or should we begin where we left off minus the perceived infidelity and the fact that I'm wealthy?"

She slid from the stool, took his hand, and led him to the bedroom.

"Forever starts here," she said.

He raised his hand. "I have another question."

"Another one?"

He nodded. "Yes, but this is my last." He pulled off his shirt and moved toward the bed. "Where are those jars of chocolate?"

Chapter 26

DANIELLE - ONE MONTH LATER

A perfect month passed. A month of sleeping in James' arms and waking up to hot coffee and kisses. He sent so many flowers her neighbors left casseroles with condolence cards thinking someone had died.

There had been death, but it was a good passing. It was the demise of doubt, despair, and devastation. And after death came a rebirth.

Life blossomed in her little cottage. She made space for his clothes next to hers and cleaned out a drawer in the bathroom for his razor, deodorant, and shaving cream. His beer sat next to her wine in the refrigerator. His Erector Set sat on the coffee table.

Each day he created something. Mostly odd-shaped hearts and words like love and bliss. He tossed her coffee maker and replaced it with a better machine that did just about everything but paint her nails.

Life was sweeter than the quarter cup of sugar she had with her caffeine. Everything was bolder, livelier, fresher. Even the floral chintz pillows in the living room seemed brighter as if the fabric had sprouted fresh buds and new leaves when he moved in. James didn't need a mansion. He said all he needed was her. God, she loved that man.

She had about ten minutes before he returned from the site to pick her up. Flynn prepared a new menu in The Lodge, one of the higher-end restaurants in the resort, and they were his first connoisseurs.

With a coffee in her hand, she walked into the kitchen and sat on the stool. In front of her lay the cookbook that started it all.

As silly as it seemed, making that cake brought James into her life. He was there as part of the corporate takeover, but she was certain he came into her life for a purpose. He was the sugar that made things sweeter. The salt that gave her life flavor, and the flour that bound her heart to his.

Baking that cake taught her to embrace mistakes. Looking back, she could honestly say that everything she'd been through, even Chris, was a lesson about love. It was the trials and errors that taught her the most about herself. Without failures, there would be no way to measure success. She wouldn't have fully appreciated what she had in her life without that cookbook. Adelaide Phelps was more than a baker. She was a sorceress of love.

Danielle touched the worn cover and traced the red heart. She laughed at the smaller letters that read, *For your eyes only.* There were rules with this book, just like in life. You had to pay attention to the details. It wasn't wise to skip to the good stuff because the good stuff was also the journey.

She desperately wanted to read the other stories but refused to press her luck. She knew the sharing part of the book was next. It was time to pass on Adelaide's wisdom. She read the preface again. It directed her to turn to the last page where she was told to open the envelope. She feared if she didn't follow the rules exactly, she'd lose everything she'd gained. Danielle Morgan had never been superstitious, but she wasn't taking any chances now that she had everything.

The envelope wasn't sealed, and she took out the single page and read the previous baker's words.

To find love, you must love yourself first.
Iris

Below, it told her to jot down what she'd learned or a few words of wisdom on a new page and put it in an envelope for the next baker.

It instructed her to sign the last page and secretly pass the book to someone in need.

"Are you ready?" James called from the front door. He no longer knocked since he had his own key.

"Almost." She wrote a message on a clean sheet of paper, put it into a new envelope, and tucked it back into the pocket. She straightened the note she found and stuck it to the refrigerator with a magnet.

James walked into the kitchen to find her staring at it.

"To find love, you must love yourself first," he recited. He wrapped his arms around her waist and set his chin on her shoulder. "Who's Iris?"

Danielle turned around and lifted on tiptoes to kiss him. "I don't know, but she's right." She wiggled out of his arms, picked up the book, and tucked it inside her purse. "I'm ready."

THEY ARRIVED at the restaurant hand-in-hand. It wasn't the first time they were together as a couple. Since James' admission, he retired his undercover boss routine. At the unveiling of the new Luxe sign, he came clean with the staff about his position and their relationship.

The funny thing was, no one questioned her authority or why she got the job. Her record spoke for itself. It didn't hurt that James told everyone she was the boss of his heart.

They snaked through the restaurant and found Allie waiting at a table alone.

"Ah new love..." she sighed when they approached holding hands. "I'd settle for old love. Hell, I'd settle for any love."

"Sounds like time for a trip to Heartbeat," Danielle turned to James. "This time, you're invited."

"Wouldn't matter. You're my girls, and I protect what's mine."

Allie stuck her finger in her mouth and made a gagging noise. "Really? You're torturing me with your love."

Her phone rang. When she looked to see the caller, she groaned. "And the hits keep coming." She pointed to her screen. "Sorry, but I have to take this if we intend to serve food at the resort." She disappeared around the corner.

James stood. "Should I tell Flynn we're here?" He turned toward the kitchen door but didn't move.

With his back to her, Danielle tucked the book into Allie's open bag.

"He knows we're coming. While we wait, you can provide the appetizer," she said.

He took his seat and leaned in. "What's on my menu?"

She loved the heat of his body. The gravelly tone of his voice did crazy things to her insides.

"How about we start with a kiss?" She pressed her lips to his, expecting a peck and nothing else, but the kiss was one of those drugging ones that left her yearning for more.

When they parted, James looked at her with tenderness. "How is it that every kiss is better than the last?"

She leaned into him, resting her head on his chest. "Because we know that every kiss could be the last."

His arms wrapped around her possessively. "Someday, I hope Allie finds a love like ours."

She glanced at the old book that peeked out of Allie's bag. "I think her luck in love is about to change."

Sneak Peek of A Pinch of
Passion

Someday, someone is going to look at me like I'm everything they've been searching for their entire life...

That was the entry Allie Parks had written in her planner on January first, when all responsible people wrote down their wishes and dreams ... right after they planned their year and outlined their professional goals. Possibly after highlighting monthly meetings and putting in daily accountability targets. As the chief operating officer of Luxe resorts, she had little wiggle room for failure.

She sat at a corner table in the dining room and glanced around the space. It was an upscale lodge with its high-timbered ceilings, antler chandeliers, and wood inlayed walls depicting all the major mountain peaks in Colorado.

She flipped through the pages until she reached June and checked off the items she'd accomplished that morning. She might not have found her prince, but she'd resolved the linen problem. She touched the frayed tablecloth and heaved a sigh of relief.

At Wharton School of business, she had a professor who never stopped talking about the Pareto Principle and how it held true for just about everything in life. But it didn't work here in Timberline, Colorado. She'd exhausted eighty percent of her time and energy to get twenty percent satisfaction, rather than the other way around, but at least it was resolved—no more see-through towels, threadbare sheets, or frayed table linens.

She'd resolved it with good old greenbacks. In her experience, most people were motivated by money, and Starr Linens wasn't an exception. They'd dug in their heels until a lucrative deal was settled upon. It was more than she hoped but less than she was willing to pay.

"Negotiating linen costs is not the hill I want to die on." She checked that item off her list, and looked up from the dining table just in time to see her brother, James, lead his girlfriend, Danielle, through the Lodge. It was the restaurant Allie hoped would earn them enough accolades to put them on the culinary map.

While linens were important, food was tantamount to success. A Luxe resort wasn't luxe if the food wasn't Michelin star worthy.

"Ah, new love..." she sighed as they approached holding hands. "I'd settle for old love. Hell, I'd settle for any love."

"It sounds like time for a trip to Heartbeat," Danielle turned to James. "This time you're invited to go clubbing with us."

Allie laughed. She was glad Danielle and James had worked out their differences and realized that their love was the only truth they needed to know. Before seeing her brother with Danielle, she wouldn't have believed there was a perfect love for anyone, but James was genuinely happy he'd found "the one."

James pulled out Danielle's chair and took the seat next to her. "An invite to Heartbeat would matter as much as it did the last time. I'd come regardless. You're my girls, and I protect what's mine." He leaned over and kissed Danielle square on the lips.

Allie stuck her finger in her mouth and mimicked gagging. "Don't torture me with your love." She wasn't generally a busybody, but after James and Danielle broke up, she played her hand at being cupid just once, and it seemed to work out. She'd lured them both to Heartbeat, the hottest new club for pickups, and then disappeared, leaving them to figure it out on their own.

Her phone rang and she looked at the screen. "And the hits keep coming," she groaned. "Sorry, but I have to take this if we intend to serve food at the resort." She jumped up and walked around the corner into a private dining room.

"Allie Parks," she answered.

For the next ten minutes, she heard every reason from out of stock, to out of season, for why she couldn't have what she wanted when she wanted it.

"How much is it going to cost me?" she asked.

The man on the other end spouted off a ridiculous percentage increase.

"Not on your life. I'll pay three percent and the expedited delivery charges. Take it or leave it." She hated it when people thought they could bulldoze her. She might have been petite at five-foot-three, but she had the inner strength and fortitude of a T-Rex.

She hung up and headed back to the table. The *clickety-clack* sound of her heels against the tile flooring echoed through the almost empty dining room.

"Sorry about that." She checked off another item and closed her planner. "We're squared away on linen and produce."

Danielle, or Dani as her brother had nicknamed her, bounced in her seat. "That's wonderful news. How did you get the linen guy to acquiesce?"

Allie sat up in her chair and smiled. "I told him I'd meet him in the alleyway on delivery days for a quickie."

James's jaw dropped open and Dani cocked her head.

"Kidding. I simply offered him more money. Obviously, I hit the sweet spot, or I drove him batshit crazy, and he agreed to the deal just to get rid of me." She picked up her planner and stuffed it into her bag. "How about lunch?"

No sooner had she sat down, when Flynn, the kitchen manager, walked out with a bottle of red wine.

"Good afternoon. Thanks for coming in to sample the new menu. I've paired today's choices with a nice dry red." He poured a splash into James glass and waited for his approval. James swirled, and took a drink before passing the glass to Dani.

After a sip, she said, "It's not Pride Reserve, but it's better than boxed wine."

When he went to pour Allie a glass, she shook her head. "None for me, I've got to hit the road soon." A feeling of giddiness welled up inside her. "I'm looking at a place to live since I don't have a boyfriend I can crash with." She eyed her brother, who'd recently abandoned living with her at their father's vacation home to move in with Dani. "I need to get out of Dad's house. It's too big and lonely to stay in all by myself."

"You can move into the little apartment attached to my office until you find something," Dani offered.

James shook his head. "No, she can't." His eyes pleaded with Dani. "Sometimes, that's the only place I can go to steal a kiss from you."

Allie watched her brother and Dani interact. They were two halves to a whole. Would she ever find her perfect half or was she already too much on her own?

Flynn's sous chef, Mollie brought arrived with the starter, and set the tiny plates in front of them.

"To start, we have wild salmon tartare with sungold tomatoes, haricot vert, and pressed cucumber with a tomato consommé."

"Fancy," Allie said and took a bite. "It's good, but what sets it apart from the other fine dining experiences in Timberline?"

Mollie laughed. "There are no fine dining experiences in Timberline. You have to cross into Aspen for that."

"True," James offered. "But what makes us different from anyone within a hundred-mile radius?"

Mollie stood taller and pressed her hands down the front of her blinding white chef's jacket. "Everything is organic. We purchase locally when we can. Just wait until you get to the main course. I've got a venison steak that will melt in your mouth."

"Oh good, wild game." Allie smiled and tried to not look like she might get sick. She'd rather eat canned pet food than gnaw on a piece of venison. It didn't matter how it was cooked, deer meat never tantalized her taste buds.

"I'll be back in a few minutes with the second course," Mollie said.

As soon as she was gone, Allie reached for her bag. "Sorry to eat and run, but I've got to get to the place I'm trying to buy."

"Where is it?" James pushed away his nearly empty plate.

"It's off of Pine Bluffs in a building called Evergreen. Get ready because I'm sure it will need some of your magic." Her brother was a master craftsman, and he had the skills to turn a piece of coal into a diamond in record time.

He pointed at her. "Are you wearing that?"

She stood and looked down at her Chanel suit and Louboutins. "What's wrong with the way I'm dressed?"

"Nothing." He shook his head. "Just hand over your checkbook and let the realtor write in the amount she wants. You can't negotiate a fair price when your shoes probably cost more than her mortgage."

He had a point. She glanced at her watch. If she hurried, she could make it back to her father's and change into something nice but didn't say empty my bank account.

"You're right. I'll change, and then head over."

"Take Dad's old Jeep instead of the Porsche."

"You make me sound awful with your brand shaming."

He shrugged. "No use arriving with a neon, flashing dollar sign that says I can pay whatever you're asking."

"Whatever." She dismissed him with a wave of her hand. "You two be good," she said moving past them. "Let me know if the menu is up to par."

She rushed home. As she approached the house, she laughed. Her father who spent his summers on the golf course in Palm Springs, called it their winter cabin, but it was twelve thousand square feet of pure luxury, not the tiny stacked log structure that the word cabin implied. The only reason he kept the place was because her mother didn't get it in the divorce, and it was paid for.

She raced inside and changed into black slacks, a pink silk blouse, and Kate Spade loafers. She refused to dress down completely. There had to be an entry point to the multimillion-dollar building, and she didn't want to appear under-qualified either.

The little detour to change her clothes put her behind schedule. She climbed into her father's old Jeep. Old wasn't quite accurate. It wasn't even out of warranty, but it had seen some four-wheeling, and had a road hard look about it with its scarred rims and dented quarter panel.

She whipped down the long winding driveway and turned onto the highway. If she pushed the limits, she could make up a few minutes and be on time. Someone once told her that early was on time, and on time was late. Though she always had a lot on her plate, respecting other people's time was important.

Reaching to grab the lipstick in her purse, she swerved and slightly crossed over the line. The car coming her way laid on the horn and offered an unpleasant gesture. She overcorrected sending the Jeep into a fishtail and causing her heart to skip a beat at the near miss.

"No shade of red is worth dying over." She took a few deep calming breaths, but her heartbeat jolted when she saw the flashing red lights in the rearview mirror.

"Not now." She mentally counted her most recent ticket and wondered how many points she could lose on her license and still be allowed to drive. "How fast was I going?" she asked out loud. She looked down at the speedometer and realized she was traveling at close to twenty miles over the limit, and that was a six-point ticket. "I'm so screwed."

She slowed down and pulled to the side of the road. A thousand thoughts went through her mind, but the loudest was, *how can I get out of this mess?*

In the mirror, she watched the officer in the cruiser behind her. She knew how this went. He'd sit there a few minutes and make her sweat. No doubt, he'd run the plates to be sure the car wasn't stolen. She said a silent prayer hoping the registration was up to date.

As she waited for the officer to stroll to her window, she considered her options. She could cry, but the last time she did that, the officer handed her a Kleenex and a ticket.

She could undo another button on her blouse and try to woo him out of a citation, but most chickens had bigger breasts than she did.

She could say it was a bathroom emergency, but dysentery was no joking matter. When they'd been looking at a site in Mumbai, she experienced food poisoning. It was one of the reasons they didn't take over the property. The restaurant had been closed down several times for health violations and a resort would never recover from having the reputation of making people sick. Nope, she wouldn't lie about a bathroom issue.

She considered using humor, but the only police officer joke she knew was, *What do you call it when a prisoner takes his own mug shot? A cellfie.* That would probably get her thrown in jail for having criminally bad taste.

She could fake sick and say she was on her way home to rest, but if he looked at her driver's license it would show an address in Vail which was exactly the opposite direction she was heading.

Note to self ... update the address on my license.

She could be honest.

She watched as the officer climbed out of his cruiser. He was tall, dark and deadly, or at least his expression was. This was going to be bad—really bad.

Dear Baker

Dear Baker,

Cake, like love, is all about the ingredients but also about the effort. Both take time and patience. Like Danielle, I've loved and lost. But lessons are learned by doing. A cake never gets made if the ingredients sit on the counter untouched. Love never happens if you're afraid to open your heart. The greatest loves and the greatest desserts happened because someone took a chance on someone or something.

Every second is your forever. Why not start it with fudge cake?

Kelly

Forever Fudge Cake

Forever Fudge Cake

• 4 squares of Baker's unsweetened chocolate
  • ½ cup of hot water
  • ½ cup of sugar
  • 2 cups of cake flour
  • 1 teaspoon baking soda
  • ½ teaspoon of salt
  • ½ cup of softened butter or shortening or butter-flavored
shortening
  • 1 ¼ cups of sugar
  • 3 eggs
  • 2/3 cup milk
  • 1 teaspoon of vanilla extract

Directions

Place the chocolate and the water in the top part of a double boiler (Basically, a pan over a pan of boiling water). Heat and stir until the chocolate is melted. Don't cheat and stop before it is creamy.

That leaves chunks of Baker's chocolate, which apparently tastes like a monkey's back end. Add 1/2 cup of sugar to the creamy chocolate and cook for 2 minutes. Cool to lukewarm (Basically, when you can touch it without needing first aid).

Sift the flour with the baking soda and salt and set aside.

Cream the butter, adding 1 and 1/4 cups of sugar gradually, and mix until light and fluffy. Add the eggs, one at a time, beating thoroughly after each is added. Now add the milk and flour mixture to the creamed mixture half at a time, mixing after each addition until smooth. Last, add the vanilla extract and chocolate mixture and blend.

Bake in two greased and floured round cake pans at 350 F for 40 minutes, or until done (You know it's done if you can stick a toothpick in the center and it comes out clean). Spread the forever fudge frosting between the layers, and on the top and sides of the cake.

High altitude: Don't let the thin air make you breathless, leave that to love. For more specific high-altitude baking instructions, Google it.

Forever Fudge Frosting

Ingredients:

3 squares of Baker's unsweetened chocolate

2 tablespoons of butter because quality is important when it comes to ingredients and people.

1 ½ cups of sifted powdered sugar

½ cup of cream or half and half

Dash of salt

1 teaspoon of vanilla extract

1 ¼ cups of sifted powdered sugar, divided into thirds. Yes, there is powdered sugar twice. Remember sugar makes life sweeter.

Directions

Melt the chocolate and butter in a pan over boiling water. Blend well. Think of unmelted chunks of chocolate as monkey bottom. Add the 1 ½ cups of sifted powdered sugar, cream or half and half, and a dash of salt all at once. Beat until smooth. Place the mixture in the pan over a low flame, cook and stir until the mixture bubbles at the edges.

Add 1 teaspoon of vanilla, then add the 1 ¼ cups of powdered sugar in thirds, beating after each addition until smooth. If necessary, place the mixture over a bowl of cold water until thick enough to spread.

Get a free book.

Go to www.authorkellycollins.com

Other Books by Kelly Collins

An Aspen Cove Romance Series

One Hundred Reasons

One Hundred Heartbeats

One Hundred Wishes

One Hundred Promises

One Hundred Excuses

One Hundred Christmas Kisses

One Hundred Lifetimes

One Hundred Ways

One Hundred Goodbyes

One Hundred Secrets

One Hundred Regrets

One Hundred Choices

One Hundred Decisions

One Hundred Glances

One Hundred Lessons

One Hundred Mistakes

One Hundred Nights

Cross Creek Novels

Broken Hart

Fearless Hart

Guarded Hart

Reckless Hart

Recipes for Love

A Tablespoon of Temptation

A Pinch of Passion

A Dash of Desire

A Cup of Compassion

A Dollop of Delight

The Second Chance Series

Set Free

Set Aside

Set in Stone

Set Up

Set on You

The Second Chance Series Box Set

Holiday Novels

The Trouble with Tinsel

Wrapped around My Heart

Cole for Christmas

Christmas Inn Love

Mistletoe and Millionaires

Up to Snow Good

Wilde Love Series

Betting On Him

Betting On Her

Betting On Us

A Wilde Love Collection

The Boys of Fury Series

Redeeming Ryker

Saving Silas

Delivering Decker

The Boys of Fury Boxset

A Beloved Duet

Still the One

Always the One

Beloved Duet

Small Town Big Love

What If

Imagine That

No Regrets

Small Town Big Love Boxset

Frazier Falls

Rescue Me

Shelter Me

Defend Me

The Frazier Falls Collection

Stand Along Billionaire Novels (Steamy)

Dream Maker

Making the Grade Series

The Learning Curve

The Dean's List

Honor Roll

Making the Grade Box Set

Deliciously Dirty Novels

Just Dessert

Brownie Points

Whipped

A Deliciously Dirty Collection

About the Author

International bestselling author of more than thirty novels, Kelly Collins writes with the intention of keeping the love alive. Always a romantic, she blends real-life events with her vivid imagination to create characters and stories that lovers of contemporary romance, new adult, and romantic suspense will return to again and again.

For More Information
www.authorkellycollins.com
kelly@authorkellycollins.com

Acknowledgments

There are so many people to thank including my wonderful husband Jim who is always there to lend his support.

A big shout out to Melanie Summers who is the sun on a dreary day and knows exactly what to say at the right moment. She also helps with my blurbs from time to time, and that always feels like a lottery win.

My editing team works endlessly to take what I send them, and they rub it to a sparkling finish. Brooke, Kasi, Janice, and Donna, I'm grateful for your help. If dangling participles were a true crime, I'd be serving a life sentence.

Big hugs to my mom Joyce Collins who claims to be my biggest fan, and I'd bet she is.

Thank you to the ARC readers in both Kelly Collins' Book Nook and Kel's Belle's who are always up for a read. Many of you started as fans and have become friends.

Now to you my dear reader, thank you for taking your precious time to read my words. I hope you enjoyed the story.

Hugs,
Kelly

CPSIA information can be obtained
at www.ICGtesting.com
Printed in the USA
BVHW041747130621
609475BV00015B/720